W9-BGD-372

CHILDREN
OF TIME

CHILDREN OF TIME

Deborah Moulton

Deborah Moulton

DIAL BOOKS ▪ NEW YORK

CHILDREN OF TIME

·One·

David stood with his parents at the spaceport viewing
room and watched the departing ship through the huge
glass window. The ship was one of the New Terra
series, huge and ponderous, capable of holding one
thousand settlers as well as animals, equipment, and
supplies. The low drone of its engine vibrated the
walls and floor of the port.

In the various viewing domes David thought he
could see many faces staring back at him and at the
Earth that they might never see again. The rumbling
increased as the ship lifted slowly through the sky.

David's father cleared his throat. "When she clears

3

regulation altitude, she'll exceed the sound barrier. Then she'll gradually increase speed to a cruising mode of around one hundred thousand miles an hour. Fascinating."

"One keytop, Dad," said David, reminding him of the new speed measurements that the government was trying to introduce into the schools.

Jack Bennet affectionately ruffled his son's hair. "One keytop, indeed," he laughed. "When your mother and I were children, cars still had wheels."

Mary Bennet looked at her husband reprovingly. "You make us sound so old. Speak for yourself. I don't actually remember driving in a car with wheels. Although I saw one once. It was in the Midwest after the farming crisis. Believe it or not, I saw a truck with wheels taking hay somewhere. There were children riding on the hay. They were very dirty and looked hungry."

There was a dull rumble that spread into a roar. "There's the barrier, and she's off," said Jack cheerfully. He put his arm around his wife and kissed her gently on the cheek.

"Dad, why can't we go too?" asked David.

"Because, son, you're only sixteen years old, you have your education to complete, and besides, this is home. This is our planet. We belong here."

"We belong here. This is our planet. You're always saying that. What about the War?"

Jack smiled. "David, people have been talking about

the War and the possibility of Earth destroying herself for over a hundred years. It hasn't happened yet."

"It's just that most of my friends have gone. And
the ones that are left are always being shuffled around
to different foster homes."

Mary looked tenderly at David. "Darling, you know
that most people can't have children. Remember your
history? When they tried to rebuild the ozone layer,
the synthetics they used entered the ecosystem, and
now only five percent of the world population can
produce normal children. The Guardians have forbidden anyone with damaged genes to reproduce, and
rightly so. The human race would irreversibly mutate
within one or two generations."

"Besides," added Jack, "If everyone who carries
normal genes leaves, sooner or later the Earth will
become an empty planet. Your mother and I feel it is
our duty to stay here and weather the storm."

David sighed. It was a speech he had grown tired
of hearing. He hated being loaned out to childless
couples who showered him with presents and made
him call them "Mommy and Daddy," always hoping
he would choose to stay with them as was his legal
right. The month with his own parents was almost
up. He wished more than ever that his own family
unit would leave on a settler ship so that he could
stay with them always.

He stared grimly out the window. Now that the
ship had left, the huge runway was stark and barren.

Its surface was riddled with black scars caused by rockets and shuttles misfiring. There was a fine drizzle of rain thrumming against the glass. He watched a solitary robot sweeper zigzag mindlessly across the cement. He felt the gentle pressure of his dad's arm on his shoulder.

"Come on, David. It's time to go home."

The descending escalator was fairly empty. So at the pressure of their feet on the first flat metal step, a black chair inflated at the rail, and a static recorded voice asked politely if they would like to be seated. David sank gratefully into the soft plastic. It was a twenty minute ride down to the entrance level of the spaceport. The building had been built to accommodate thousands of travelers. David could remember when the escalator had been jammed with people crushed up against each other. Now the spaceport was deserted. It was rare to hear the click of human feet on the floor. In corners, robotic information centers waited patiently to be asked information, and electronic security beams continually scanned the empty halls and corridors.

"We are approaching the entrance level of the Constitutional Spaceport of the United Eastern Sector. Please assume a standing position, and remember to collect all personal belongings. We hope you have enjoyed your visit with us. If you need any further informational assistance, please follow the yellow . . ." The recorded voice droned on with helpful suggestions and ended with "Have a nice day" just as the metal step of the escalator merged with the floor of the entrance level.

David stood up. The chair hissed softly as it deflated and was sucked back into the railing.

Outside, the moisture-filled air blew against his face in cool waves. He breathed deeply. There was a tang of smoke and disinfectant in the air. The pavement was slick. To one side, a street sweeper began twirling its brushes as its sensors picked up their presence. David knew the minute they stepped off the pavement, the sweeper would spin to where they had been standing and scrub and disinfect the spot with robotic perseverance.

"David, you haven't adjusted your clothing control and it's raining!" Mary reached quickly inside her son's coat and turned the dial. Immediately the fabric of his clothes gleamed a dull orange to indicate rain protection. The smooth sphere of the head protector snapped into place, and he was surrounded by warmth.

"Mom, it's raining, not snowing!" he argued as he reached in his lapel and turned down the heat control.

"Well, I don't want you getting sick just as you're getting ready to stay with your foster parents. It reflects badly on us, you know, if you go there sick. Besides, *I* don't want you to get sick."

David smiled at his mother. Then he kissed her quickly on the cheek. He knew that the months when he was away from her were just as hard on her as on him. "I always come home, Mom. And I always will. Even if you try and fry me in my own clothes." He laughed as he said this. He hoped his mother would laugh too, but she hugged him close instead.

"Oh, dear," Mary said as she glanced at her husband. "I can't help wishing sometimes that we were safe on some settlers' ship."

"We're safe on Earth, Mary."

"It's not the War. Of course I'm afraid of the War, everyone is. But I hate saying good-bye to my son over and over again. And as more and more families leave, there are fewer children to share. How do we know that the government won't take David away from us altogether?"

"They'd never do that, Mary. Even the Central Computer would never make a law like that."

Mary sighed. "I hope you're right," she said slowly.

David stared at the drizzle. Far in the distance, he could see their car skirting across the deserted parking lots as it moved toward them. He knew his father stayed up late many nights studying early editions of the Constitution, that he wrote long letters to the area representative, and sent numerous applications for a personal visit to the Capital that were all denied.

Finally the car arrived. The air movers released slowly until the car rested on the street with its door open. When the Bennets had seated themselves inside, the doors slid firmly shut, and the air movers lifted the vehicle once more.

"Hello, Mr. Bennet. What is your destination?" asked the car's computer politely.

"Home," said Jack, and punched a button on the keyboard.

"Thank you," replied the computer, and the car whisked out into the empty street. As they entered the thruway, the street lights blinked on before them, and when they had passed, blinked off again. The rain, heavy now, splattered against the windows.

"Tomorrow begins a new month, David," said Mrs. Bennet. David stared out the window and did not reply. "Your foster mother is very wealthy and powerful. It's a wonderful opportunity for you. She requested you. I didn't know you had met her before."

"Who?" asked David.

"Anastasia Grey."

"I never heard of her before in my life."

Mary frowned slightly. "Strange. Maybe she heard about you on the news when you won the I.O."

"Intellectual Olympics," snorted David. "What's the use of solving mathematical equations faster than anyone else, when the computer will always do it for you, and much quicker. I only entered for a joke."

"David," said Mrs. Bennet reprovingly.

"It's that kind of attitude that got the Guardians installed in the first place. I was very proud of you

for winning the I.O." Jack Bennet's voice was stern.
David shrugged his shoulders.

"Let's not fight on your last day. This Anastasia
Grey requested you. It's quite an honor." Mrs. Bennet brushed at David's jacket and rearranged his collar. "Please be polite and remember your manners.
She has informed the school that she will have you
tutored privately."

"I won't go to school for a whole month? The
P.S.A.T.'s are coming up. I can't afford to cut school
now."

"Son, she's hiring *people* to teach you," broke in
Mr. Bennet.

"I've never been taught by a person," grumbled
David. "I'll just get embarrassed and I won't learn
anything."

"David, you don't get real teachers until graduate
school, and even then only twice a year. This will
look great on your educational résumé. First the I.O.
and now this. If she likes you . . ."

"I'm not going to stay with her, Dad. I don't care
how rich she is, or what she can give me. I'll do the
required month, and that's it."

"We love you, David. We just want what's best for
you," said Mrs. Bennet sadly.

"I know, Mom. And I know that Dad's right about
staying on earth. I just hate leaving home and pre-
tending that other people are my parents."

"It's the law, son. Remember your Constitution—

Guardian amendment three hundred and sixty-two, which ensures the right of all legally married couples to experience parentage?" said Mr. Bennet. "And fortunately, it's only for one month, unless, of course, you wish to be adopted permanently by Lady Grey."

"Lady?" asked David skeptically.

"The title was officially registered with the European Heritage Banks, bought and paid for, complete with a Latin motto: *Pueri omnia vicent.*"

David's jaw dropped. "What does it mean?"

Jack grinned. "I researched that one too. *The children conquer all.*"

Although he had spent his whole life fostering with different people, David felt a small wave of apprehension growing inside him. "Anything else about her that I should know?" he asked.

"That's all I could get, son," answered Jack. "Not much is known about Lady Grey. I tried to access her file on the general computer, but the link was denied. She's powerful, David."

"Do I still have to call her 'Mommy'?"

"That's up to her."

David sighed. The car's computer interrupted the conversation to inform them that they were approaching their destination. The car turned and skirted up the narrow driveway between the long borders of green perma-plastic hedge. As the home sensors recorded their approach, the lights in the windows began to twinkle brightly, and the living room curtains pulled back. David could glimpse the warm red of the sofa, and the glitter of bric-a-brac on the tables.

The car came to a gentle halt. "You have arrived at your destination. There is considerable precipitation with a temperature reading of fifty-one degrees. Please adjust your clothing controls appropriately. It is eight twenty-five P.M. Have a pleasant evening." The computer voice clicked off, and David stepped onto the entry porch of his home. Then the front door opened out quickly like a welcoming arm.

"Hurry, David. I don't want the rain to get on the rug. The sweeper will be at it all night, and we won't get a wink of sleep!" urged Mrs. Bennet.

As the family entered the house, the door closed and locked after them. Automatically they each glanced quickly at the communications monitor in the wall.

"No calls, and the ship got off on schedule," said Jack as he passed the unit.

"We were there, Dad. Punch up the sports, would you? I want to see how the Hawks did against the Hellions. They're three for three in the series. I hope this Lady Anastasia has a sports hook-up."

"Well, you can always get the scores on general access."

"But not the plays, Dad. It's not just which team wins the point, it's how the point is played. Besides, Nollen Franko's out with a twisted knee, and some new rookie is subbing for him. Dad, when I get back from this month's fostering, will you take me to a game, a real one? You promised last month, and then you got into all those research meetings."

Jack rested his hand on David's shoulder. Then he pulled his son against him affectionately. "Sure, David. I'll take you to a game. And that's a promise."

"Great, Dad. And I'm going to hold you to it this time."

As David snuggled into his bed and drifted into sleep, he smiled happily as he thought about attending a real game. He could hardly wait until his foster month was over.

· *Two* ·

Because David was going to be picked up directly from school by his foster mother, his dad gave him a lift. Mary had packed his best clothes in a new suitcase and, as always, hugged him, told him to be polite and that wherever he was, she loved him. Then she had turned away so that he wouldn't see the tears in her eyes. But David knew they were there. "Don't worry, Mom. I'll be back at the end of the month, I promise." As he and his father drove away, David kept his eyes staring straight ahead. He knew from experience that looking back at his mother made it more difficult, for both of them.

"She always cries when she says good-bye to me, Dad," he commented thoughtfully. "I would never choose a foster parent over her."

"She knows that, David. But the months you're away from us, she worries. Are you sick? Are you eating well? You know the law; we can't contact your foster parents. You can't contact us. Sometimes I think we should leave like the others."

"You'll never leave Earth, Dad. You'll keep trying to disarm the Guardians and bring back live government, even if you're the only one left," David said affectionately. Jack frowned and ran his hand through his shaggy gray hair.

They said good-bye on the school steps. "Remember about the game, Dad," called David after his father. Jack turned and waved cheerfully. Then he walked slowly toward the car. David watched him as he went.

His father was tall and lanky. He stooped slightly as he walked. The last few years had aged him. He works too hard, David thought. Most of the other research scientists had given up trying to disable the Guardian System and were fleeing Earth to settle new worlds. Almost everyone who could afford settler passes was buying them. Even without the threat of ultimate destruction, the synthezone radiation would linger in Earth's atmosphere for at least another fifty years. But Jack Bennet said this was where the human race evolved, and he for one intended to spend his life fighting for humanity on Earth.

For a moment David had an urge to run after his father and hug him, and tell him that he loved him and was proud of him. But the first-period indicator was beeping loudly, and he didn't want to be late for class.

As David slid into his seat, his desk screen rose and flickered. "Good morning, David. You were almost late this morning," admonished the computer voice gently. "Today's assignment begins with a historical review of Earth's major wars. I hope you have done your homework."

David sighed and inserted his homework disk into its slot. His work was displayed on the screen as the computer analyzed, corrected, and graded what he had done. He glanced about the room. Most of the desks were empty now. The friends he had grown up with had left for distant planets. He felt a hand on his shoulder.

"Hey, David—" It was Paul Quintsy. "Guess what?"

There was a faint whirring sound from the ceiling. David raised his hand in warning. "Shhh. The Central Monitor."

"Big deal. I'm going to—"

"Talk to you at recess," snapped David. The last

thing he wanted was a disciplinary communication going to his foster mother.

"Okay, Okay." Paul nodded and crept along the floor back to his own desk, carefully dodging the monitor's moving beam of light.

"David," reproved his own computer. "You must pay more attention. Your math homework was satisfactory, but I'm afraid your writing assignment leaves much to be desired. The analytical section of the Problem Solving Aptitude Test involves a considerable amount of writing. Please use the remaining minutes of this time period to construct an outline detailing the advantages of a computer-based government. By the way, congratulations on scoring so well on your physical development series. You are now ranked fourth in the national sixty meters placement."

"Thanks," muttered David.

"But physical achievements are no excuse for weak intellectual performance."

"I just won the I.O.'s, remember?"

"It has been determined that irrespective of your achievements, you are still operating considerably below capacity. The outline please?"

David groaned as a keyboard slid out from the computer and the screen wiped clean and black for his words. So much for trying to stall for time.

At recess he met Paul in the pool. The water was warm as they swam back and forth together. Overhead the monitor whirred ceaselessly. Artificial light outside the huge glass dome made the room seem bright and airy. On one wall a hologram of the sea stretched far into the distance. Waves heaved and crashed. Sea birds trilled as they swooped about the cloud-filled sky.

After they had swum, they stood under warm jets of air that dried them within a few seconds. "My dad signed for the next ship," said Paul excitedly. "We'll be leaving next month. I wish you were coming with us."

David shook his head. "My parents want to stay on Earth," he said.

"Well, your dad's an apex level scientist, and your mom's mid-top research. They've both got jobs. My dad hasn't worked in years. There's nobody left to work for."

"I wish we were going," said David. "I start a new foster month today."

"No more foster months for me. I'm headed for the stars!" crowed Paul.

"Pretty soon, I'll be the only one left here." David fastened his jacket and checked his temperature control.

"Nancy Stevenson will be back. She's with her mom in the lunar facilities while her mom has the new baby."

"Mrs. Stevenson's having a baby?" asked David.

"It was all over the news. It's the only baby being

born this winter in the Eastern Sector. She's isolated
in the Lunar Hospital so that Earth's atmosphere can't
contaminate her."

"My mom did that with me," commented David.
"She said it was boring up there."

"It's law now. They can't afford to take any chances.
Who are you fostering with this month?"

"Lady Anastasia Grey."

"I've heard of her. She's supposed to be very rich.
Not bad, Bennet. It could move you into a government position if she adopted you permanently."

"Sorry, Paul, but as soon as this month's up, I'm
going back home. My dad's promised to take me to
a Hellion's game!"

They walked back to their classroom, talking about
their favorite sport, dimensional hockey. It was almost like old times, except that the halls of the school
were empty. Occasionally they passed another student going to a different wing of the building. Then
they would wave and call out. With so few children
in the educational complex, which had been built to
accommodate thousands, everybody knew everybody
else's name. David wondered if soon he would be the
only student in the huge school. He would miss Paul.
And, for a whole month, he himself would miss school.
This thought frightened him. He had never had a
human teacher before. What if when he returned to
school everyone had left on different star ships? He

would never get a chance to say good-bye, and he would be alone in the Plexiglas halls, and the holograms of forests and meadows, with no one to talk to.

"You really should leave, David," Paul said earnestly. "My dad says there really will be a war any day now. And if there is, everyone will be killed and Earth will become a radioactive wasteland."

"My parents will never leave," said David. He shook his head sadly. "Paul, I should say good-bye to you now. Anastasia Grey is going to have me tutored privately by—" he swallowed hard—"people!"

"Real human teachers?" asked Paul incredulously. "I didn't know there were any left."

David nodded. "But it means I can't go to school this month. Today's my last day. A car's picking me up after classes."

"I'll miss you, David," said Paul.

"I'll miss you too. Have a safe journey to wherever your ship takes you."

The two friends shook hands. Then with a laugh, they embraced each other. David felt very sad. He would miss Paul. There was only one other student in his class, Willard Patterson. And David had never liked Willard at all.

When classes were over, David walked slowly down the shimmering metal steps. He hoped he would see other students before he left, but the school grounds were empty. In the distance he saw Willard. "'Bye,

Willard," he yelled. Willard turned and waved. He began to walk toward David, but at that moment a tall man dressed in seamless black approached.

"Mr. David Bennet?" he asked in low, formal tones.

David clutched his suitcase firmly. "Who are you?" he asked.

"I am the Lady Anastasia's chauffeur, Sarke," said the man, bowing slightly. The way he said his name reminded David of one of the few remaining types of fish in the Earth's oceans—fish with sharp teeth that preyed on each other, and even on human swimmers. The man took David's suitcase. "Come with me, please, Mr. Bennet."

David followed hesitantly. He turned and saw Willard staring at him.

The car was large and black. There was a thick, sweet smell coming from its interior. It had no windows. David paused and looked back at the enormous school structure gleaming white and silver on the hill. He wished he could run away from the black car and the chauffeur who stood like a guard behind him. He had the feeling that this foster month was going to be very different from anything he had ever experienced. Trying to appear calm, he nodded at the chauffeur and stepped into the vehicle.

"Make yourself comfortable, Mr. Bennet," said the chauffeur calmly. "I think you will find everything you need."

The door of the passenger compartment slid shut.

Inside the car resembled an elaborately decorated
chamber. There was a soft rug on the floor, and a
reclining chair. Fresh flowers were arranged in vases,
and on the wall were several oil paintings in heavy
gilt frames. A heavy metal plaque set with large semiprecious stones was recessed into the wall. It showed
two stags, skewered on the same spear, and the words
Pueri omnia vicent.

The children conquer all, thought David as he settled himself uneasily into the car seat. The soft silk
cushions enveloped him with heavy perfume. He
looked for a communications monitor but saw only
carved wood. Finally, he banged on the front wall.
Immediately one of the pictures dissolved into glass,
and he saw the stony face of the chauffeur looking at
him. "I was looking for the communications monitor," he said apologetically.

"There is none," said the chauffeur. "If you require food or drink, there is a compartment to your
left. If you require bathing, I will arrange a tub. If
you require assistance, please ring the bell to your
right."

"Are there any general access films?" asked David
tentatively.

"There is no monitor. However, I will arrange a
music program which I believe you will find most re-
laxing. Have a pleasant journey, Mr. Bennet." The
window became a picture again. David had the un-
easy feeling that he was being observed continuously.

He leaned back in the chair and tried to appear calm.
He wished he had asked how long the trip would
take, but somehow he didn't want to see the expressionless face of the man working the car's computers.

Soft music began to play in the background, a flute
blended with a piano to create an eerie rippling mel-
ody. The air smelled heavy and thick. David wished
there was a window to look out of, or that the compartment was cooler. He found his eyes aching with
tiredness, and every time he forced them open, he
stared either at the holograph behind which sat the
chauffeur or at the metal plaque with the dying animals. It was easier to sleep. He shut his eyes, and
the silk cushions seemed to rise up and smother him
with warmth and perfume.

When David awoke, he was lying flat. There was
a cool softness under him, and a gentle breeze was
blowing in his face. His eyes were strangely heavy,
and his body felt as if he had forgotten how to move
it. He lay motionless. Finally, his eyes opened. He
was in a large bright room. The ceiling reached up in
a marble arch, and there were narrow slits of windows
stretching up to the top of the dome like ice fingers
on glass. He wondered if he was in an ancient church
of some kind. There was no sound. He was covered
with a soft silk sheet, and his head rested on an embroidered pillow.

"How do you feel?" The voice was friendly. David
turned and saw a girl about his own age sitting beside

him on a velvet chair. She was dressed in a long rose-colored skirt, and around her head was a fine gold band. She looked as if she belonged in a medieval painting. Her hair was long and golden.

"Where am I?" he asked.

"I think you are strong enough to walk," the girl answered, which was not really an answer at all.

"Are you Lady Anastasia?" David asked.

The girl laughed. "No, I'm not. But you'd better call her 'Mommy' when you meet her. She can get very angry."

"Am I dreaming?"

"You're not dreaming, David."

"You know my name?"

"Of course."

"What's yours?"

"Irene. Come on, it's time to meet Mommy now."

David sat up. The room began swimming. He felt Irene take hold of his arm. He saw to his horror that he was dressed in what appeared to be a long white nightgown that was belted with a heavy golden cord.

"Where are my clothes?" he asked as he staggered to his feet.

"Mommy destroys all things from the outside world."

"She destroyed my clothes? What am I going to tell my mother, my real one, when I get back?"

Irene didn't answer him. Instead she said, "Here, lean on me. After you walk around a bit, you'll feel better. Mommy wants to meet you, and she doesn't like to be kept waiting."

David stood up cautiously. He took a few steps across the room and found he was leaning heavily on the girl's shoulder. The floor was cold against his bare feet. "Have I been drugged?" he asked. "My legs feel numb."

"I know, but it passes. We'd better hurry."

David could sense the tension in Irene's voice. He nodded and, gripping her shoulder, followed her out of the room.

The hall was empty. Its white marble walls stretched up very high. Here also the ceiling was arched. David heard a sudden flapping of wings accompanied by gurgling coos. The noise was strange and echoed eerily. He glanced up apprehensively. He could not tell whether the birds were above him or in another chamber. The corridor seemed to go on forever. David felt his legs and arms becoming strong again. He took his hand off Irene's shoulder.

"Feeling better?" she asked. He nodded, startled at how loud her voice sounded. Irene grinned. "It's okay, we're allowed to talk," she said. "Now David, we're almost at the Great Hall. I know this is really new to you, but we've all been through it. Just stand up straight and speak clearly, and *please* remember to call her 'Mommy.' "

They had come to the end of the passageway. In

front of them towered two huge metal doors elaborately carved with vines and unicorns. The doors were
locked shut. Irene stood back and looked at David
critically. Then she straightened his long white tunic.
She passed her hand over a small grinning face in the
carving. The heavy doors began to open, silently and
slowly.

"Good luck," whispered Irene as they entered a
huge room.

· *Three* ·

The Great Hall was silent. On either side were rows
of children, mostly younger than David or Irene, all
dressed in strange medieval clothes. At the far end of
the room, on a tall stone dais, sat a woman with flaming red hair and very white skin.

"Go on," whispered Irene. She gave David a small
push. He walked slowly up the aisle, following a narrow red carpet that ran the length of the room and up
the stone steps. He had never seen so many children
in his life. The room began to swim and his legs began to tremble. Somehow he knew he must not fall
down.

The Lady smiled. "Welcome home, David," she said huskily. Her voice was deep and echoed through the room. She was wearing an embroidered gown that reached the floor and a white velvet cape that covered the first several steps.

"Hello, Mommy," David said with cautious formality. He stood at the foot of the steps. Never in all his many months of fostering had he ever encountered as bizarre a situation as this. How had the government allowed this woman to collect all of these children? The law was specific, one child per couple, per month. None of this made any sense. His head began to ache as his body struggled to overcome the drugs in his system. Surely this was part of a dream.

"These are your brothers and sisters. My darlings, your manners, please."

"Welcome home, David," said the children in unison. The noise of their voices thundered in the marble hall. Startled, David glanced at the row upon row of white faces. He did not see the Lady signal with her long pale arm, gather her robes, and disappear through a small curtain at the back of her platform. When he turned toward the chair again, it was empty.

He felt a tug on his arm. "Come on, David. You can go back to your room now." It was Irene. "You're probably still feeling a bit sick from your ride. Don't worry, it passes."

The children filed out of the room. "You did very well, David. I think Mommy is pleased with you. A lot of the children cry and carry on when they realize they're not going back to their old lives."

For a moment David was too horrified to speak. "I'm only here for a month," he finally managed to say.

Irene looked at him with pity in her eyes. "No, David. You're here for the rest of your life. We all are."

"Not me," said David firmly. "I don't know what's going on here, but I'm going to find out, and in the end, I'm going home."

"David," Irene's voice quavered slightly. "David, this is your home. And I'm your sister."

"Sister?" said David belligerently. "Sister? I've never seen you before in my life. This is not my home, and that lunatic lady with the red hair is not my mother, not in a million years!"

"I'll take you to your room now," said Irene calmly. "The castle's pretty big. You might get lost."

David followed Irene down the long corridor. He wondered where the other children had gone. Except for the flapping and cooing of the pigeons far above him, the hall was silent. Irene paused and ran her palm along a portion of the wall. Immediately, the outline of a door became visible. David realized that "Mommy" used holograms like everyone else. Somehow this reassured him. He nodded curtly to Irene as he passed inside.

"I'm not your enemy," the girl said.

"You're not my sister either," said David as he shut the door firmly behind him, leaving Irene alone in the corridor.

David sat on his bed and looked around the room. Whatever drug he had been given was indeed wearing off. The room was not nearly as big as he had thought when he first awakened. Neither was the ceiling so high. There was a window in the far wall. He pulled aside the heavy brocade curtains and peered out. He could see nothing but meadows, fringed with forests, and beyond that mountains. However, there was no way of knowing whether this vista was real or a hologram. His own parents refused to use synthetic window views. He could hear his father's voice saying patiently, "They're not real, David. I want to look out my window and see what's there."

"It's only the hedge and the front yard, Dad," David had replied. All his friends had synthetic views. Their windows revealed the shore pounded by waves, or deserted western canyons.

"Yes, son. But it's our hedge and our front yard. And if by chance a bird visits our yard, we'll see it. And we can watch the leaves on the tree turn colors in autumn and drop off, and come back again in spring."

He remembered replying, "You can get all that with a hologram, Dad."

Now David sighed. He could see his father had been right, and he wished he could tell him so. "I've got to get out of here somehow," he said aloud. The government could not fault him for escaping, especially when he'd alerted the authorities to the vast number of fosterees Lady Anastasia Grey was hoarding.

He continued his examination of the room. His bed was in the center of the floor on a low marble platform. He tried to move it, but it was either too heavy or else it was fastened to the floor in some way. The sheets were a glistening white silk. The single window was too narrow to climb out.

There were two other doors beside the one that led to the corridor. One opened to a closet, which was filled with the same type of medieval clothing in which he had been dressed, and the other opened to a sumptuous bathroom. This room was almost as large as his bedroom. The walls were marble, with golden tiles running in bands around the perimeter. The bathtub was huge and sunken. There were potted ferns in the corner, which, to David's surprise, were not holograms, but real plants.

He wondered if the whole adventure so far had been a dream, and he would wake up as the black car pulled in front of an ordinary house, with an ordinary woman rushing out to meet him. He shook his head. Ordinary women did not have chauffeurs. If it was not a dream, was he then really a prisoner? Cautiously he crossed the floor and pushed his finger along the seam of his door.

It opened silently. The hall was empty, but dark and ominous. Somehow the room, strange as it was, seemed safer and more familiar. He shut the door and returned to the bed. It did not seem as if he was a prisoner. Maybe at the end of a month he *could* return to his own parents. But where did all the other children come from? Why was the Lady Anastasia permitted to have hundreds of children? Or had she somehow stolen them?

Somewhere a gong sounded. The vibrations were deep and melodic. David glanced at the walls for traces of speakers but could find none. The gong was struck again. There was a tap on his door.

"It's me, Irene."

David opened the door. Irene stood before him in a beautiful rose-colored velvet gown that trailed behind her.

"I've been assigned to show you around," she said. "It's dinner now." Her voice was uncertain, as if she expected him to be angry with her.

Instead he smiled. "You look really pretty, Irene," he said, and meant it.

Irene blushed. "Thank you." Then she glanced at him and gasped. "David, you're not dressed for dinner. You're still wearing your initiation garment. Mommy will be so angry with me!"

David could see she was genuinely frightened. He had fostered with a few mothers who had been violent. He knew that some foster parents believed in harsh punishments. "Don't worry, Irene. You won't get into trouble. Just show me what I should wear, and I'll get dressed quickly. Mommy will never know."

"Oh, we'll be late," gasped Irene. She flew across the room, opened his closet, and pulled out one of the more elaborate costumes. It was a dark blue velvet, studded with semiprecious stones that glinted and sparkled in the light.

"This has got to be one of the most weird foster months I've ever had," said David conversationally. He wished Irene would lose her scared-rabbit look. But instead she began pulling the garment off its hanger. "Don't *ever* let Mommy hear you talking like that," she said frantically. "Here, put this on!"

"Do you mind?" asked David as Irene began unfastening his initiation tunic.

She blushed. "I'm your sister," she snapped. "And we're already late."

David folded his arms stubbornly.

"Oh, all right," Irene said as she pivoted on her heel and glared angrily at the wall.

"Don't worry, I'll be dressed in no time." David said reassuringly. He quickly threw off his tunic and pulled on the blue velvet pants, the jacket with the stones, and the lace collar, and buttoned it up quickly. "How do I look?" he asked. Irene turned. She shook her head. "And you've forgotten your circlet," she said, as she rushed across the room and opened a drawer in the closet that David had not seen. She grasped a thin band of gold and placed it on his head.

"Now, come on!" she said, and grabbing his arm, pulled him out of the room and down the corridor.

"In all my months of fostering, I've never had to wear costumes for dinner," David said cheerfully as he ran beside Irene. His self-confidence was returning as he realized the absurdity of the situation. "I can't wait to tell Paul about this one. He's my best friend at school. Well, my school's almost empty now. So I guess he's my only friend."

"David, you've got to stop talking like this! You'll get us both in trouble!" said Irene, panting as she increased her speed.

"What I can't understand is how you *chose* to live with this fruitcake over your own parents," said David as he lengthened his stride easily to keep up with hers.

Irene stopped suddenly and yanked him back. "Will you shut up?" she hissed. "This is the dining hall. Walk in calmly, and for goodness' sake, smile at Mommy!" She ran her hand over the wall, and a large door appeared in the marble. The door slid silently open, and the sound of children's laughter and the flickering light of torches spilled out into the corridor.

David and Irene entered the dining hall. The talking and laughter broke off as every face turned first toward them, then to Mommy, who sat at a table on a platform above the rest. In back of her stood the strange chauffeur.

"David and Irene, my darlings, you're late for dinner," said Mommy reprovingly. Then her voice softened. "But it's your first night, my child. And you look very handsome in your dinner clothes." She studied David critically. The room was silent. David lifted his chin and stared back at her evenly. "Yes, yes, my darling boy, that blue velvet sets off your blond hair very well, and you have strong shoulders and a good build. Traditional bone structure, that's what I like to see in a boy. You may sit by me this evening and tell me what it felt like to win the Intellectual Olympics and prove yourself physically as well. I think we have the perfect catch, Irene."

Irene blushed and turned away.

Imperiously Mommy beckoned to David. "Well, don't dawdle. Sit beside me in the place of honor."

"All right," answered David cautiously. "Mommy," he added, when he saw her begin to frown.

"And Irene, you join us," said Mommy graciously.

David and Irene walked up the steps to the platform, and Lady Anastasia gestured for them to sit one on each side of her. David looked down and saw row upon row of children sitting at long benches, all staring up at him with pale faces and big eyes.

"Carry on, my darlings. I like the sweet sound of your little voices," said Lady Anastasia.

The children began talking again, and the room

was filled with the sound of forks clinking against plates, and laughter. The chauffeur brought Irene and David plates of food. David stared at the slice of meat, which was very rare, and watched red juice puddling out from it on the white china. There was a vegetable he could not identify, but it looked a bit like spinach, although it smelled of burned carrot.

Lady Anastasia put her hand on David's arm. Her fingers were white and cold, and her nails were very long and painted red. She wore several large rings.

"You must eat, my child," she urged. "You are a growing boy."

Irene leaned over and sent David a warning glance. "Yes, Mommy," said David obediently. He began to cut the meat and wondered why Irene was so frightened. Finally, he laid down his knife and fork, cleared his throat, and addressed his foster mother. "Look, Mommy, I don't understand what all this is about. You live in what appears to be a castle, you have hundreds of children, and you make everyone wear strange clothes. I'll do my best this month to fit in with your household. However, when this month is over, I'm going back to my own parents and my own house, and not you or anybody else is going to stop me. I know the law, and I also know my rights."

The room had become silent again. He glanced down and saw the terror reflected in the children's faces looking up at him. He knew it was bad form to mention his own parents when he was assigned to a foster home, but at the same time, he wanted to set the record straight. He would call this strange lady "Mommy" for a month. He would wear strange clothes. He would even eat raw meat, if his foster mother insisted. However, he would only do it for a month. After that he was going home. His dad had promised to take him to a live Hellions game. Besides, no "Mommy" could ever even begin to take the place of his real mom.

The Lady began to laugh, first low, then high and shrill. The children followed suit, and soon the room was noisy again.

"David, my darling son," she said when her laughter subsided. "There is so much you don't understand. I am the only mother you will ever have, because I am the mother that will save you from Earth and its destruction!"

David felt a sinking in the pit of his stomach. "I'm still on Earth, aren't I?" he asked in a low voice.

"Of course, my sweet son. You will *inherit* the earth. When the foolish nations have destroyed each other in war and there is nothing left, you, my darling children, the children of time, will go forth in innocence and conquer this wasted planet. In the end, you will build a paradise from the ashes. And I will be the divine mother of a new race!"

·*Four*·

Jack Bennet stared at the communications monitor in disbelief. Was it the fiftieth time? The hundredth time he had done this, hoping for a miracle, hoping for a different answer? VERIFY. DAVID BENNET, ADOPTION STATUS.

AFFIRMATIVE, came the answer again. LEGAL A-DOPTION BY LADY ANASTASIA GREY.

He switched to audio-mode.

"Yes, Mr. Bennet," said the computer's voice politely. "David Bennet, your biological son, has chosen to remain with Lady Anastasia Grey. This transaction has been approved of by the Central Computer and at the wishes of David Bennet, according to the constitutional law, amendment number three hundred and sixty-four, which clearly defines free choice of parentage as relating to fostering. If you have further questions, please cross index foster-ing—amendment number three hundred and sixty-two, as approved by the Guardian Computer's enrichment and clarification of the Constitution of the United States of America, following the general intent of our country's Founding Fathers in the year 1787. Thank you, Mr. Bennet, and have a nice day."

"Jack?" Mary's voice was concerned. "What's the matter? I just came in and found you staring at the monitor. Are you all right? The sweeper's on the fritz again. It started vacuuming my feet when I entered the house. We'll have to get a team in from Central to adjust it, although I know how you hate drawing attention to the house. But we can't have the sweeper attacking people like some sort of rabid animal. What's wrong?" She hurried over to Jack and rested her hand gently against his chest.

"David's been adopted." Jack watched Mary's face become pale. Almost angrily, she rushed to the console and began typing the same sequence that Jack had. And always the same answer appeared, quickly and politely, leaving no room for doubt.

He hated seeing her like this. "Mary, I've been at it all afternoon. It's no use."

Finally, she stood with her hands limp at her sides. "I'll never see him again," she said. Jack put his arms around her. "We'll find out more about this Lady Anastasia," he said. "She's bound to have a file somewhere! I'll get access. I promise."

"And then what?" asked Mary bitterly. "What can we do? According to the amendment, we're not his parents anymore!"

Jack felt a wave of rage sweep over him. "We are

always his parents, Mary," he said angrily. "We'll find him. We'll get him back!"

"But what if he's chosen her over us?"

"He wouldn't choose foster parents over us. You know that as well as I. There's been a mix-up somewhere, perhaps deliberate. I have a terrible feeling that David may be in great danger."

· Five ·

"You see, David," explained Irene when dinner was over, "Mommy thinks the War is going to destroy Earth, and so she's saving all of us so that when the radiation clears, we can start out all over again!"

"She's crazy," muttered David. "Irene, I've got to escape from here."

"Nobody's escaped from here, David. A lot of children have tried, especially the ship children."

David had a sinking feeling in his stomach. "What do you mean, 'the ship children'?"

"The settler ships leaving Earth. Mommy has some sort of arrangement with the crews. Once the ships are in space and the settlers go into hybe, the children, some of them at least, are put in z-pods and sent back to Earth. Mommy has a scavenging team that picks them up. When Cory and Tanya came to, they thought they had been captured by aliens. They tried to escape. Now they're like the rest of us, they just accept it."

"What about the parents on the ships?"

"By the time they wake up, hundreds of light years may have passed. On Earth, their children and grand-children will probably be dead."

"What about your parents, Irene?"

She shrugged her shoulders. "They're dead. A mining accident in the Northern Sector."

"I'm sorry."

"It happened when I was very young. Mommy adopted me. I've lived here ever since."

"Don't you think all this is a little weird? These clothes, this castle, and this preoccupation with the end of the world?"

"I don't know. I haven't seen the outside world."

"What about school?"

"Mommy teaches us. Sometimes Sarke." David frowned in perplexity. "Sarke brought you here. He's an eleventh level scholar. He's taught at real universities. He's also a master of the ancient defense arts. He's Mommy's servant," she added.

David turned from her and paced across the room. He stared out the narrow window at the fields far below him. The scene never changed, but he still wondered if what he was staring at was a hologram. There was a lot he needed to find out about before he could make his escape. He didn't feel he could trust Irene completely, not yet. "All right," he said slowly. "I'll do my best to fit in, at least for this month."

Irene smiled happily. "Oh, David, that's all Mommy wants, is for you to try."

"You'll have to help me, though. I don't know what to wear, and I don't know my way around this place." David had expected Irene would be reluctant to show him the castle, but instead she smiled.

"Mommy was so right about you. She says that there's no substitute for basic intelligence combined with basic physical strength. It makes you a survivor."

"Huh?"

Irene smiled. "And a leader. Now, finding your way around the castle is simple. Mommy hasn't given you a study schedule yet, so you'll have lots of free time on your own to explore."

"Even outside the castle?"

Irene shrugged her shoulders. "Of course," she answered. "You're not a prisoner here. Tomorrow I'll show you the castle and the stables."

"Stables?"

"Of course. Can you ride?"

"You mean horses?" asked David incredulously. He had seen them in the nature preserve area of the park. But it never occurred to him that people still learned to ride the animals. It sounded dangerous—not something the Central Computer would approve of.

Certainly it violated some safety code. It was against the law to knowingly endanger yourself.

Irene nodded. "You'll learn. Mommy loves horses. Sometimes she calls the castle her ark. She will save the children and the horses. I have things that I must save too."

"What?" asked David.

"I have wonderful secrets, but I can't tell anyone, not even you. You'd better get some sleep, Brother."

"Good night, *Irene*," said David firmly.

Irene melted into the corridor. David could hear her long velvet skirts swishing over the cold stone. Then she was gone.

He shut the door and paced around his chamber. He wondered what Irene meant when she said she had secrets. What did she mean about the horses?

The light had faded to a soft golden. Outside the night was black. David wondered what time it was. There was no clock or communications monitor of any sort. He went into the bathroom and filled the enormous carved tub with the steaming scented water that shot out of two goblin heads. The steam made heavy cloud patterns in the marble room. When he emerged, he saw that a long white nightshirt had been laid on his bed. Someone must have snuck into his room while he was bathing. Was he being monitored? He squinted at the walls, then hastily pulled the shirt over his head. It was soft and warm against his skin. Suddenly he was very tired, so tired he could scarcely move his limbs to the bed in the center of the room.

When he woke, the room was filled with light. It was morning. He stretched luxuriously.

"Good morning, my darling little David." The Lady Anastasia was sitting in a chair by his bed. Her eyes were violet in the morning light, and her hair curled out in all directions. David felt suddenly cold. "I have been watching you sleep. I like to watch my children when they sleep." The Lady smiled at him.

"Good morning, Mommy," said David cautiously.

The Lady laughed long and merrily. "And you are wondering, my sweet little boy, whether you should kiss me on my cheek as a show of filial affection. That's good. I like to keep you wondering. My little boy blue. You know the nursery rhyme?

> *Little boy blue, come blow your horn,*
> *The sheep's in the meadow, the cow's in the corn;*
> *But where is the boy who looks after the sheep?*
> *He's under the haystack fast asleep."*

David sat up slowly. "I'd like to get dressed now . . . Mommy," he added. For her face had become suddenly menacing.

The woman shifted in her chair. As she rose, the many jewels embroidered on her long robes clattered together. "Today you must start your studies, my sweet lamb."

David glared at her. He did not like his foster mother's habit of calling him "sweet" or "lamb" or "little boy blue." He almost growled, "My name's David!" But as he looked at her, he felt a dull knot of fear tightening his chest. There was something very scary about this woman. Instinctively he knew it would be dangerous to anger her.

"Irene will help you with your schedule, my pet." Lady Anastasia swept out of the room, leaving a smell of jasmine hanging in the air. David shivered and waited for the gentle tap on his door that would mean Irene had come.

He wondered what his studies would consist of. As yet he had seen no communication monitors. Would Mommy herself teach him? Would Sarke? Were there other adults in the area he had not met? Would any of them help him escape?

Irene brought with her a white, coarsely woven garment consisting of pants and a loose shirt. She double-tied a thick white belt about his waist. "Sarke will teach you combat," she explained. "First body combat, then weaponry. I guess the tour of the castle will have to wait."

"Martial arts?" asked David. "Why? Computer force fields will always protect me, protect anybody, unless the War comes, and then we'll all be dead anyway. Besides, it's against the law to use the human body as a weapon."

"I don't know anything about the laws out there."

Irene frowned and she tightened his belt. "But here there are no force fields to protect you. You have to learn to protect yourself."

"From what?" asked David.

"You'll be tested. We're all tested. You never know when the tests will come. Please learn all you can from Sarke."

David nodded. He wondered what his father would say. His father had always told him that knowledge was good and that learning only made you stronger. Very well, he would learn what Sarke had to teach.

He followed Irene through the long stone corridor, down a winding staircase, and finally into a huge white room. There were no windows. The floor was covered by a white canvas mat that made the bottoms of David's feet feel itchy. Sarke came toward him. He was dressed in white also, but around his waist was tied a black belt. He smiled down at David.

"Good morning, Master David," he said. "I suggest we dispense with the customary formalities and get straight to the point."

Before David could reply, he found himself lying flat on the mat groaning with pain. He tried to catch his breath but his stomach burned, and his lungs refused to expand.

"Is this how we learn our lessons? Lying on the floor?" asked Sarke. He smiled a tight smile and gave David a sharp kick. David winced and staggered to his feet. "You see, little boy blue, there are no force

fields to protect you here. There are no security ro-
bots to prevent you being hurt or even killed. You're
soft. You have been raised soft. Little Alan, who is
only six years old, could kill you. Master Alan," called
Sarke. A small boy, also in white, came across the
floor. Blearily, David looked for Irene, but she was
not there.

"Master Alan, this new boy needs a lesson."

The boy nodded and walked toward David. David
looked down at the small child. "You must try and
fight me," piped the little voice.

"I don't fight children," said David between gasps.

Sarke folded his arms. "Let the lesson begin, little
Alan."

Again David found himself on his back clutching
his stomach in pain.

"Shall I kill him?" asked the small boy dancing
about. "Shall I kill him, Sarke?"

"No, Master Alan. This is not a test. Merely a lesson for our little boy blue."

Sarke helped David to his feet. "Don't worry, Master David. I will teach you well."

David spent hours in the white room. Sarke showed
him how to kick and punch and spin past his opponent in a death whirl. At the end of the afternoon he
was so tired that he made no objection when Irene
fetched him and told him to dress for dinner.

He sat at a table with the other children and looked
up at the dais where Mommy sat, attended by Sarke.

After dinner he returned to his room and fell asleep almost immediately.

He woke with every muscle aching. There was no diagnostic monitor in the bathroom and no heat probe. He took a hot bath instead, and let the heat of the water soothe his pain. Unfortunately the relief was only temporary and he hobbled to breakfast. There were several bruises on his face where he had been thrown on the hard mat.

He spent the day again with Sarke. Lunch was brought to the white room so that his studies would not be interrupted. There were times when he fell asleep on the white mats, only to be roused again by Sarke.

This regimen continued for several days. David was never sure how long. There were no clocks and no monitors. There was no way of keeping track of time or even days that passed. He felt his body begin to get strong and hard. Sarke made him do exercises to strengthen different parts of his body.

He remembered dimly, through a fog of pain and exhaustion, the exercise machines at school that moved your limbs for you. That life, already, seemed far away.

Then came a turning point. David's muscles gradually stopped hurting. He could work all day with Sarke without collapsing on the mats in sleep. After dinner he practiced the exercises Sarke had shown him. He invented exercises of his own. The bruises on his face healed. But he was determined to teach

Sarke a lesson, the same kind of lesson he had been taught on his first day.

"Ah, my little boy blue, you've been working hard," said Mommy one day. She brushed the hair back from his forehead with her long, cold fingers.

David stared at her. "I think my month here is o- ver, Lady Anastasia," he said. "And I would like to go home now."

The lady looked at him with her violet eyes. David wondered if he would be punished for not calling her "Mommy." However, instinctively he felt that a month had passed.

"But my darling boy, you've only been here a week. I'll forgive your little mistake this once. But," her voice became hard and steely, "don't let it happen again."

David clenched his fist and glared back at her. He knew she was lying. Lady Anastasia looked back at him steadily, waiting for him to challenge her, but this time he remained silent.

· *Six* ·

Jack stared moodily out the window at the tree. He felt his wife's gentle touch as she rested her hands on his shoulders. "I'm getting nowhere," he said. "It's been over a year now, and I can't access anything about David or Lady Anastasia. And time is running out."

Mary nodded. "I know," she answered slowly. "The last ship leaves in two weeks. The general public doesn't know, but there are no more ships in the spaceport, and there are none being built either. Are you going to the meeting this afternoon?"

Jack nodded. "I have to. It's our only chance. It's the Earth's only chance."

"I'd better stay here."

Jack looked up at her curiously, the familiar hope flooding through him. "Do you really think you are?" he asked.

Mary smiled and nodded.

"Darling, you're in research. Can't you just test your own blood to be sure?" asked Jack tentatively.

Mary put her finger to her lips and rapidly shook her head. "Central Computer monitors all experiments," she said softly and quickly. "A human blood sample from a pregnant woman would trigger all sorts of alarm bells. I'd be whisked off to the lunar facilities without even a chance to say good-bye to you."

Jack was silent. He knew as well as she that when the destruction came, the lunar life support facilities would be disconnected. If Mary were there . . . He tried to smile reassuringly. "You're right, Mary. We'll just have to make our decisions based on your intuition and your body signs. Think of what a surprise we'll have for David when he comes home."

It was Mary's turn to be silent. She rested her hand protectively across her flat stomach and looked out at the tree covered in the pale green of early summer.

The time came for the meeting. According to plan, Jack programmed his car to take him to the public park system, the northeast entrance, number seventeen. He knew the other scientists were arriving at the park at slightly different times and different entrances so as not to alert the sensors to an unusual amount of human traffic. The car dropped him off, politely wished him a nice afternoon, and whisked off to park itself in one of the huge municipal lots, now barren wastelands of concrete and carefully drawn parking spaces.

Jack walked carefully along one of the walks that wound its way through meadows filled with flowers. Once a deer bounded across the walk, and once he glimpsed a father and son playing ball on a field in

the distance. Again, the emptiness of being without
David. "I'll take you to a Hellions game when you
get back," he muttered to himself. Poor David. Dimensional hockey was a thing of the past now. There
weren't enough players left.

He knew that his footsteps triggered sensors, os-
tensibly for the robotic sweepers to clean up after him.
But every bit of information fed into the Central
Computer, and from there, into the Guardian. Although the Guardian had been installed supposedly
to safeguard the American governmental system and
ideals, Jack felt the Founding Fathers would roll over
in their graves if they knew their Constitution now
had nine hundred and twenty-eight amendments
making the original document meaningless.

He turned quickly into a grassy knoll. There were
no sensors in the grass, primarily because the animals
tended to dig them up and chew on them. He knew,
however, that his departure from the walk had been
duly noted by the Central Computer.

It was a beautiful afternoon. There were several
people walking aimlessly in the park area. This was
not so unusual, although the number of people was
slightly higher than normal. The number was analyzed by the Central Computer as being at the upper
end of the norm, but not requiring further investiga-
tion.

Finally, at the appointed time, by a natural outcropping of rocks, they met, twenty-four scientists from around the world.

"Vladimir, Vladimir you rascal!" said Jack warmly, grasping his best friend with both hands. The two men embraced.

"How goes it with you, Jack?" asked the older man. "And your Mary?"

"We think she might be . . ." Jack patted his stomach.

"No. I don't believe it. Has she been tested?"

"We can't take the risk."

"Of course, of course. I asked a foolish question. But David, how is he?"

Vladimir saw his friend's face and immediately became serious. "He's not? . . ."

"Dead? I don't think so. But he has disappeared. He fostered with a Lady Anastasia Grey, about a year ago, and hasn't returned."

Vladimir rubbed his face with his hand. "Anastasia. That is a familiar name. No, not just because of the old myth. It is a recent name, but right now I can't place it. Give me time, my friend."

The meeting was called to order. One by one, the scientists spoke on how they had each tried to disarm the Guardian System in their own countries. One woman had even led an armed force against her Guardian Capitol. As expected, her troop had been wiped out, and she was lucky to survive undetected.

"But what are we going to do?" asked Vladimir. "The last ship leaves in two weeks. We all know that. There will be room for us because we are scientists. The Guardians want us to leave. But what about the other people, the rest of our citizens? This Guardian System is crazy. Protect the ideals of each nation. But what about the people? I ask you, what about the people?"

"Some of my people have decided to stay," said Sharon Weisman. "And I also." She smiled sadly. "I guess when you've fought so hard to defend your right to the land, it's hard to leave it behind. Who knows, perhaps God has another miracle for us."

"How will you survive the destruction?" asked Jack with real concern.

"We have begun constructing shelters. It is complicated, Jack, very complicated. We can't use anything but the most primitive portable computers to make decisions about radiation and oxygen needs, food and water. And we must work without the knowledge of our Guardian. But we have started."

"In my country also, splinter groups have started plans."

"How long do we have left?" asked the scientist from Germany.

Dr. Yokimo spoke up. "A year at most, my friends. I have analyzed the Guardian communications, and the countdown has already started."

There was no real surprise at this. It was what everyone expected.

Vladimir patted Jack's arm reassuringly. "Don't worry, Jack. To every problem there is a solution."

"But what?" whispered Jack. "And how long will it take?"

"God only knows," said Vladimir with a characteristic shrug of his huge shoulders.

Jack grinned. "You're supposed to be an atheist, remember?"

"There are no atheists in foxholes. I read that once in one of your books. Well, Jack, the world is in one hell of a foxhole now, isn't it?"

Dr. Yokimo clapped his hands for order. "This is our good-bye to each other," he said. "Tonight, when we meet at the Annual World Scientist Conference, we will be expected to maintain our nationalistic differences."

"Good," whispered Vladimir to Jack. "I'll get to throw a glass of wine at you."

"You'd better not," laughed Jack.

"Well, I guess this is good-bye then," said Vladimir. He embraced Jack fiercely, and Jack found himself clinging to his friend as if he could not bear to let him go.

There was crying and hugging all around. A silent but unanimous decision appeared to have been reached—not to mention the last ship. But Jack knew that most of them, with the exception of Sharon Weisman, would leave.

He walked slowly back to the northeast entrance to the park. He did not retrace his steps exactly, as that would have been suspicious. So he had no way of knowing whether the boy and his father were still playing ball in the field.

"Well?" asked Mary when he entered the house.

Jack shook his head. "No progress. Yokimo says the countdown has begun. We have a year, maybe less, before the end."

Mary rubbed her stomach thoughtfully. "I'll stay with you, of course," she said.

Jack looked out at the tree, his tree. It was growing dark now, but he could still see the outlines of its branches against the sky. "I have to stay, if only because of David. But it isn't just you anymore—it's—" he rested his hand on top of hers.

"But will it be safe to deep-hybe when I'm—?"

Jack nodded. "Yes. Research has been done. The fetus hybes at the same rate as you. Besides, the top medical scientists will be there to monitor the process until stasis is reached. It's customary for the scientists to be the last to enter hybe and the first to break hybe at the end of the journey. You'll certainly be among friends. They all know this is the last ship. We said our good-byes at the meeting."

"There's still the conference tonight," said Mary gently.

Jack tipped back his head and drew a deep breath. "Yes, a show meeting," he said bitterly. "So that the Central Computer can see that we still have our nationalistic differences. We have to stand around and glare at one another. It's ridiculous to have to pretend with my friends."

"Perhaps if you showed the Central Computer that this friction between our nations no longer exists, the Guardians would call off their ridiculous war!" cried Mary.

"That was tried," said Jack angrily. "Two years ago, remember? The three scientists who tried it disappeared for 'psychiatric adjustment'! And they haven't been seen since! The Guardians *want* us fighting. It's part of their programming. I would call in sick tonight, but that would only draw attention to you. We can't risk the baby."

It was the first time Jack had thought of his wife's pregnancy as a baby, a baby inside of her, growing bigger and stronger every day. Up until now it had been "the fetus." All of a sudden, it was a baby. For an instant all of his worries about the Guardians and the War and even David, vanished. And he wrapped his arms around Mary and felt her warm against him.

All too soon, the last day came. Jack drove his wife to the spaceport. She carried only the small regulation bag issued for space travel. In it she had put her favorite hologram, an image of David and Jack stand-

ing under the tree in the yard. Jack knew she had
also packed a small stuffed bear, which she had had
as a child and treasured all of her married life. There
was no room for anything else. She would have taken
the house if she could have fit it in the bag. She had
even said good-bye to the robotic sweeper that she
had sworn at on so many occasions.

The crowd outside the spaceport was enormous!
Somehow word had got out that this was the last ship.
Thousands of people were screaming to be let in. Jack
had never seen so many people. He didn't realize
there were that many people left on Earth. He felt
Mary nervously touch his arm.

"I'll call security on the car communicator," he said
reassuringly as he stopped the car a safe distance from
the crowd.

The security vehicle glided slowly through the
rioting people. Jets of steam were shot at the ones
who tried to attack the vehicle or hang on its sides.
Jack stroked Mary's head as she turned her face into
his jacket in fear.

The tank carried them straight through the main
doors and into the building. "Please dismount, Dr.
and Dr. Bennet," said the robotic voice politely. "And
check your seats for any personal belongings that you
may have left behind."

As they stepped out of the security vehicle, Jack
could feel Mary's fingers tighten on his arm. The
spaceport was filled with people frantically rushing

about. A metallic voice issued from a speaker. "There are five minutes to final embark sequence. Please have your boarding passes ready, and report to gate fourteen on the second level. Thank you."

"Getting here took longer than I thought," said Jack as he guided Mary through the crowd. "But we're okay. Got your bag?" Mary nodded.

They reached the second level. Soon they were at the gate. Beyond this point, only Mary would be permitted.

Suddenly she dissolved into sobbing. "Jack, please let me stay with you. I can't go. Or come with me! There's still time. They always want the scientists to go. It's wrong for us to be separated."

Jack winced. The pain inside him was almost unbearable. "We have David to think of," he said, trying to keep his voice level. "I've got to be there for him. And it's not just you anymore, Mary."

Suddenly, Jack felt a heavy hand on his shoulder. He turned quickly. "Vladimir!" he said in surprise.

"Yes. And you are coming on the ship?" asked the burly Russian.

"I'm staying. But Mary is going."

"Oh, I see." Vladimir looked at Mary thoughtfully with his clear gray eyes. "That is the right decision. Hey, cheer up," he patted her clumsily on her cheek. "It's not good to get upset in your, you know . . . Besides, you'll be perfectly safe and among friends. The whole gang is going."

"All the scientists?" asked Jack.

"Well, everyone except for you, and you have David to find yet . . . and of course Sharon, who's still convinced her people can survive another holocaust. Don't worry, Jack, I will personally supervise Mary's situation. And sometime, way in the future, we will be saying a prayer for you, Mary and I and the little Bennet. Perhaps I'm not an atheist anymore. We'll see."

Mary tried to smile through her tears. She turned to slip her pass into the gate log.

Suddenly Vladimir clapped his hands to his head. "Oh my God, Jack, I almost forgot. I managed to get some information for you. I don't know if it will help. Remember the Reverend Joshua Sarkoman, who was charged with drugging his congregation, conducting strange killing rites, and trying to conquer the world?"

"Incarcerated on a rehabilitation satellite, sixty years ago, shortly after the installation of the Global Guardian System," said Jack quickly. Time was running out, and he wanted to hold Mary close to him one last time.

Vladimir shook his finger. "Well, a certain Lady Anastasia Grey intervened. He was released into her care and was never seen again!"

Mary turned to Jack. "Oh, darling. I love you," she said. "Please tell David I love him. I know you'll find him. I know you will."

"Come, Mary Bennet," said Vladimir gently. "We don't want to miss our ship."

"Good-bye, Jack," called Mary frantically as Vladimir pulled her down the long corridor.

"Good-bye, I love you," Jack cried out.

It seemed to Jack he was waving and calling long after Mary and Vladimir had disappeared from sight.

Countdown began. From the viewing dome, Jack watched the steam pour from the launch pad. Outside the wire fence hundreds of people pressed frantically toward the ship. The fence gave way, and they ran to the rocket, climbing its burning surface with their bare hands. Some reached the ship, and even as the ship lifted off, were banging helplessly on the sides of its portholes.

Then the doors of the building collapsed, and the corridors became full of angry people. When they realized the ship had indeed lifted off, they became crazed, attacking and smashing whatever lay in their path.

Dazed, Jack picked his way quietly through the mob. "Now I have to find my son," he whispered.

But what did Joshua Sarkoman, the mass murderer, the self-proclaimed specialist on mind-altering drugs, the religious fanatic who butchered hundreds of innocent people, have to do with Lady Anastasia Grey? What did it all mean? And where did David fit in?

·*Seven*·

David entered the combat room alone. He was to be
tested. That much he knew from Irene. But why did
she seem so terrified?

With a swish of her silver cape, Mommy appeared.
Behind her filed the children, in silent rows. The
children sat cross-legged around the edges of the room,
staring at David. He knew most of them now. He
knew of their terror of Mommy, and how they cried
late at night for homes they were supposed to have
forgotten. The bright velvets and satins of their medieval clothes made them seem younger and more
vulnerable than ordinary children. Yet every day, they
were drilled on riding formations and battle combat.
Even David had learned to ride.

"My darlings," said Mommy in her piercing voice.
"We are here to test David. He has studied with Sarke
for over a year, if we were counting outside time; but
of course we're not, are we, my children?"

"No, Mommy," the children said in unison.

"As you know, I test to weed out the weak. I want
only strong children, very strong children for what lies
ahead."

"Yes, Mommy," murmured the children obediently.

David felt the room spinning. A year? How could a year have gone by? Two months, perhaps. A year? How had the days been divided? Was that why there were no clocks in the castle? How could the Lady Anastasia alter time like this? Or was she lying?

"If I fail your test, will you send me home, to my parents?" asked David hoarsely. He stared ahead as he fixed a picture in his mind of his house and the tree on the lawn, his father hunched over the communications monitor writing letters to the government, and his mother laughing with delight over a change in particle currents that were displayed on her electronscope screen. Somewhere the Hellions were playing or practicing on their multileveled arenas. Tickets were easier to come by now that Earth was almost empty. When it rained, his mother always turned up the heat on his climate control dial. She would reach impatiently inside his jacket with a frown. It was always the same frown. But what if his parents had left? What if they thought he was dead? Or worse, had chosen this crazy woman over them?

"David, dear boy," said the Lady Anastasia, her lavender eyes glinting and her red hair almost sizzling against the white wall of the gym. "Dear boy, why do you keep up this fantasy, this delusion of another home? This is your home. I am your mother. But

even a mother must be strict sometimes for the good
of her family. If you win, you live."

"And if I lose?"

"You die."

David glared at the woman with true hate. "Not
much of a choice, is it, Lady Anastasia?"

"Meet your opponent, my dear," said the Lady,
and she rubbed her pale hands together gleefully.

David spun around. In back of him stood a black
form. Sarke!

"Master David," said Sarke evenly.

"I don't understand," faltered David.

"It is a fair match," said Lady Anastasia. "Sarke
tells me you are a very good student. He will enjoy
killing you. I like him to enjoy himself now and then.
Or maybe you will kill him. That would be an inter-
esting lesson."

David felt his heart begin pounding. His muscles
seemed weak and numb. He knew he didn't stand a
chance of holding out against Sarke, let alone winning.

Lady Anastasia held her pale arms above her head.
"Let the test begin," she said in a loud voice.

David felt a searing pain in his chest as Sarke planted
a well aimed kick. He dropped to the floor and rolled
quickly to gain his breath. Sarke lunged after him.
For a moment the dark face loomed over David. David
kicked out, trying to snare his opponent with his

knees, but Sarke threw his own weight back and broke the hold. David knew Sarke was heavier and stronger. But he also knew that he was slightly quicker. If only he could use this to his own advantage.

For what seemed like hours, David was able to dodge and dance around the older man. But he was tiring. The floor became slippery with sweat. A few trickles of blood slid into his left eye. Somehow his head had gotten injured in the fight. He blinked and tried to focus through the red. Sarke swung at him. He stepped back. A searing pain shot through his leg as his ankle turned and his leg crumpled under him. Sarke struck several quick punches at his chest.

David sank to his knees and half-heartedly raised his arms to block the deadly attack. He knew he would die. He would die in this white gym in front of these children in their medieval costumes, and in front of the witch who insisted she was his mother. He would die with Irene watching. He felt no pain as Sarke kicked him repeatedly.

Why don't I hurt anymore? he wondered. What's happening to me? His mind drifted back to his home, his father listening to him talk about school. "We studied dying today. Sometimes, you don't feel any pain, just calm and accepting. It's chemicals released in the brain. Isn't that incredible, Dad? Isn't it?" David forced himself back to the present. Am I dying now? he asked himself.

He almost wanted to feel afraid and bring back the excruciating pain of his ankle. Worst of all was the thought that he had lost to Sarke. It seemed to make his life pointless.

He tried to fix the picture of his parents in his mind. Somehow, if he could see them as he died, he would feel victorious, if only for a moment. He heard Sarke's maniacal laughter on the edges of his consciousness.

Lady Anastasia rose. "Just like old times, Sarke," she said in a clear, cold voice. "But I remember the treatment in the correction satellite! You were screaming and begging."

For an instant, Sarke's face became blank. He stared motionless into the air, his mouth lax and his eyes glazed.

David forced himself into consciousness. If he had a chance, this was it. He rolled backward, summoning every inner reserve of strength. His body was slick with sweat, and the sound of his own breath was loud and raspy. If he missed, he would be dead. There would not be another chance. But if his kick found its mark, maybe . . . But why did the Lady help him? What did she want from him?

He gritted his teeth and shot his foot toward Sarke's face. His heel scraped hard across the man's eyes. Sarke staggered back. He groped for David's foot, trying to slam him senseless to the floor! Temporarily blinded, he snatched futilely in the air, and in that second David staggered to his feet, raised both fists, and smashed Sarke to the ground.

"Kill him, David," said the Lady in a soft voice. "Kill him now, or one day he will kill you."

David stood panting with his hands clenched tight. Every muscle in his body throbbed in pain. His ankle seemed to explode in agony, and his stomach knotted in wave after wave of nausea. There was a slippery scum on his face that he knew to be blood. Every fiber of his body hated Sarke. In spite of the pain in his leg, he felt his tendons begin to stiffen and his body summon its reserves for a kick to Sarke's chest that would terminate his dark life forever.

"If you kill him, you will pass the test," wheedled the Lady. David's hands dropped to his side.

In his mind he saw his father watching him. He remembered his gentle idealism and his profound respect for anything living. Oddly, the image of the tree in his yard passed before his eyes. He turned and faced Lady Anastasia. "No," he said. "I prefer to pass my own tests."

"You are a fool, my little boy blue. Next time I may not be able to help you. For Sarke, I think, would like me dead as well." She gave the prone man a calculating smile. Sarke did not smile, but stared with hatred as David left the room.

David did not return to his chamber. Instead, he climbed to the upper walkway of the castle—an open

space at the very summit of the mountain on which
the castle rested. Here the grass had been cropped
very short, and small flowers grew in intricate patterns. About the garden was a series of stone arches
through which the wind blew. Most of the children
hated the walkway. The wind was cold, and the
mountain seemed to drop straight down for miles and
miles. The fields and forest below looked like a distant pattern of green and gray. Although there was no
way of knowing if the vista was holographically induced, David felt it was real.

He wanted to be alone. The past few days, or had
it been months, had been condensed into a grueling
torture of training his body. Indeed, he had thought
of nothing else except to be the strongest and the
best at the ancient skills that Sarke taught. He sat on
a stone ledge and looked out. How much time had
passed in the castle? Mommy had said one year. But
was she lying? It could be more than one year. It
could be ten years, or it could be less. There was no
way of knowing. He wondered if he would ever return home. Part of him wondered if home actually
existed. Perhaps he had always lived at the castle.

David felt a gentle hand on his shoulder. It was
Irene.

"Mommy has a celebration planned for you in the
great hall," she said softly. "I knew you would pass
the test."

David turned on her sharply. "Have I been here a year?" he asked.

Irene looked away before answering. The wind blew cold and sharp against their faces. "I don't know, David. Time is different here than outside. I don't even know how long I've been here."

"How old are you, Irene?"

"I'm sixteen. But I was only six when Mommy brought me here. She chose me for something special. I can't tell you. Your work here is to learn to fight and rule. I have a different job." She glanced down at a small blue flower she was holding and twirled the stem slowly.

"When were you born?" persisted David, trying to turn the conversation back to the information he needed. He already knew Irene was different from the other children, that her studies were separate.

Irene shrugged her shoulders. "I don't know," she answered.

"What about your parents?" asked David.

"I don't really remember them. I remember them talking about the crops failing because of the ozone. And then we moved so my father could get work near the mines. I remember my father yelling at supper. He threw his plate of food onto the floor. I was scared. Then he cried. It was about the President resigning, and there weren't going to be any more presidents or leaders of countries, just a lot of computers making all the decisions. I didn't understand what he was talking about."

David stared at Irene dumbfounded. "Irene, the termination of the presidency, the farming disaster, that happened over sixty years ago!"

Irene tossed back her head defiantly. "You're lying, David! It can't have been that long ago. Mommy said you would try and trick me like this! I hate you!" She threw down the flower she had been holding, caught her breath in a sob, and ran to the spiral staircase. David watched her disappear down the stone steps, her long rose-colored skirt fluttering behind her. Absently, he picked up the flower and held it loosely in his hand.

·*Eight*·

Every evening after dinner Lady Anastasia read aloud to the children. They lay sprawled around the great hall on mats and pillows. Often the younger ones slept. The enormous fire crackled in the stone fireplace and made dancing shadows on the walls. The slender windows were black from the night outside pressing in. Lady Anastasia's voice would shriek with glee as she read truly frightening passages from an early edition Bible about hell and the demons below. Sometimes she read from late twentieth century scientists who described in detail what the world would be like after a nuclear war. David was glad the smaller children slept. The world that Mommy described would surely give them nightmares if they listened. He scanned the room protectively. Somehow he would have to get these children to safety. If only to preserve them from being exposed to such frequent hybernation.

Furthermore, he was becoming more and more certain that they were being drugged. There was no other explanation for this continued amnesia regarding the outside world. Sometimes their eyes were glazed, and even their movements were slow. David had begun sneaking drinks from the gold faucet in his bathroom so that he would not drink the spiced wine. But he was sure the spice was in the food also. What was going on here? He automatically counted the heads of the children. Someone was missing. "Where's Alan?" he hissed to Irene.

"Who?"

The boy who had challenged David at his first lesson was missing.

"Alan," repeated David.

"There's no Alan here," murmured Irene as she raised her hand to her mouth in a warning gesture.

"Yes, there is!" repeated David louder.

Several children lifted their heads and stared at

David. Irene nervously smoothed her long velvet skirt about her ankles. "He did not pass his test."

"He's dead?" asked David incredulously.

Irene nodded. "But you're not supposed to mention his name—*ever*. There never has been an Alan here, at least not that Alan. Now please, we're going to get in trouble!"

It was too late. Sarke's tall figure loomed up in front of them. He took Irene's hand. She darted a frightened glance upward and then at David.

"It wasn't her fault," said David loudly. Lady Anastasia stopped reading. The room was quiet. Some of the children began to raise their heads from their mats and look about apprehensively.

"Come, Mistress Irene," said Sarke.

"Where are you taking her?" asked David desperately. "I was the one who talked!"

"She has been rude, my little boy blue. Irene must be punished. It hurts me more than you could know, to have to punish my darling children." The Lady Anastasia sighed and placed her hand on her chest. Her red hair sparkled and glinted in the firelight. Her arms were white, but her fingernails were long and red. Sarke began leading Irene away. David rose to his feet, but Irene shook her head.

The Lady laughed long and shrill. "You see, my darling David. You are very precious to me. I won't punish you just yet for your naughtiness, but I must punish someone. It's only fair. So I punish Irene in your place. Do you understand, my dear?"

Horrified, David nodded slowly and sank back to the floor.

"Do you understand, dear?" repeated the Lady.

"Yes, Mommy, I understand," David said hoarsely. Anything, anything, to keep Irene from further punishment!

The Lady smiled. "Good," she said sweetly. "And now I'll continue reading."

The children lay their heads back down on their mats and pillows, and once again David heard the droning words about a world where only grass grew and rustled in radioactive winds, and the only things that survived were insects. David did not see Irene again for a long time.

The next day, when he was looking over the wall of the castle, he met a new teacher, Triad. Triad was a very tall man with taut, wiry muscles. His skin was glistening ebony with a pattern of pink scars disfiguring his right cheek. He had black, sunken eyes. He seemed to appear from nowhere and moved silently and fluidly across the sheared grass of the upper walkway.

"So you are the new favorite, and your name is David," he said critically.

"Who are you?" asked David cautiously.

"They call me Triad."

"What do you want with me, Mr. Triad?"

"Just Triad will do, Master David," answered the man with a thin smile. He lunged at David with a bright knife. David blocked the knife arm easily and twisted it up sharply behind Triad's back. The man winced and dropped the knife. "Sarke has taught you well," he said ruefully.

"And I have taught myself, as well," answered David shortly. He released Triad's arm and picked up the knife. It was razor sharp and glinted in the sun.

"Keep teaching yourself then, Master David, and keep learning as well. I am here to teach you survival. I will teach you how to find water in the desert and food in the wasteland. I will teach you how to read the stars like a map, and I will teach you to kill. We will start by climbing down the mountain."

David felt a rush of excitement that was almost immediately replaced by a feeling of fear. Triad walked quickly across the lawn and slid easily through one of the arched windows. David followed. It seemed the man was able to crawl down the cliff like a large fly.

"You must seek crevices with your feet. I am going before you. Mark my path."

"What happens if I fall?" asked David apprehensively as he scraped one leg over the stone balustrade.

Triad did not answer.

The two reached the bottom of the mountain by nightfall. It had been a long, slow, and tedious descent. David's velvet clothing was torn. His hands were bleeding, and his left ankle ached where he had twisted it. He was hungry and thirsty. Far above him, the distant castle twinkled with tiny lights in the black sky.

"You wish you were back there, all warm and safe?" asked Triad.

David glanced at his companion. "No," he said shortly.

"You have a lot to learn, Master David. It won't be easy, but at least the nights spent outside the castle will be honest nights. The sun will rise each morning, and each morning you will be awake. And I will teach you how to survive in the real world, the world of yesterday and the world of tomorrow." Triad's words had taken on a strange intensity.

"This isn't the real world, Triad!" David snapped angrily. "Any more than it is in there." He waved his hand at the castle. "In the real world, I live in a normal house with a communications monitor. And I wear normal clothes that keep me dry and warm and self-repair when they're torn. Not like these costumes!" He gestured angrily at the torn, dirty velvet of his sleeve. "And if I'm hurt, I call it in on the monitor, and immediately a medicart is sent to the house with diagnostic equipment and a full robotic team. I have

a mother and a father whom I love very much and
I've got to get back to them. This forest, this castle,
this is *not* the real world!"

"Your real world is ruled by computers. You're soft,
and you're spoiled," said Triad contemptuously.

Suddenly David realized, without asking, that Triad
belonged to the secret cult of Survivalists, strange no-
madic people who believed they could survive the
final War by living off the land. It was a bizarre cult.
Even the Central Computer was unable to control their
movements. And if one was caught, that person always turned on his or her own knife with lightning
speed, preferring death to questioning.

The man's voice was calm. "And now, Master David, let us gather some wood for a fire."

David woke in the morning with little memory of
how he had fallen asleep. The dawn was damp and
cold. The fire beside him gave a warm charcoal smell
but no heat. It had gone out in the night. His muscles were stiff, and the scratches on his hands ached.
He staggered to his feet and fell back with a gasp of
pain. The ankle he had sprained had twisted under
him. He rubbed it gently with his fingers. Triad was
nowhere in sight.

David sighed. If he were in the castle, he would at
least be clean and warm. However, he instinctively
felt, as Triad had said, that only one "honest" night
had passed. Was Triad one of Mommy's servants? Or
would Triad help him escape?

Silently, the Black man appeared, his scars shining pink in the morning light. "It's time for the lessons to begin, Master David," he said softly.

In the days that followed, Triad taught David how to find water by digging where the moss grew greenest in the forest, how to find animal tracks and snare small animals with bits of string and sticks. He taught David how to find his way by the stars and how shadows fell, which herbs cured and which did not. In the desert that lay to the west, David learned how to trap dew for drinking water by digging a hole and laying a plastic tarp over it, with a stone weighting the middle, and a cup below to receive the precious drops. Triad showed him how to make fire in the wilderness, and carry fire by means of a single ember buried in ash. He also showed him how to cure leather for shoes and clothing, and preserve meat over a slow smoke fire.

They did not speak much. The lessons were silent. David gradually lost his habit of reaching inside his clothing to hunt for a temperature control dial. When it rained, the remnants of tattered blue velvet clung to his skin like soggy leaves in autumn. He became used to feeling cold or hot or wet depending on the vagaries of nature. His white skin became brown. As the days passed, his hair grew long and shaggy. He tied it off his forehead with a leather cord.

Sometimes on a clear night, above the tops of the trees, he could see the faraway outline of the castle glimmering with lights. However, many nights the castle was dark and dead. Perhaps everyone there, including Mommy and Sarke, was in a state of deep hybernation. David shivered as he realized that Mommy could live for a hundred years and never show her age. How old was she now?

As time went on, Triad left him more and more to his own devices. Sometimes days would pass before the Black man would appear silently from behind a tree or materialize across a clearing without a sound of warning.

As survival became second nature to David, he used the time to think. He found his mind clearer in the forest than it had been in the castle. He was thankful that his system was slowly cleansing itself of the drugs.

He decided that Mommy's land must be somehow shielded by a force field so that those inside could neither escape nor look out, and that those outside the area could not look in. He remembered from his social studies class in school that entire states in the Western Sector had been closed off due to the dwindling population. He wondered if Mommy had somehow gained control of a state and turned it into her private kingdom.

David also remembered from his studies of long ago that all force fields have doors, that they must have doors if material is to be exchanged from the outside. The food, the elaborate medieval costumes, the holograms, all this David knew came from the outside world. He himself had come through a door somewhere when he traveled in the strange black car with no windows.

So he ran. Every day he ran great distances to try and find the perimeter of the kingdom. He discovered the desert was smaller than it looked. The huge expanse of towering dunes and burning white sand was an artificially created environment. The impression of an eternity of shifting sand and empty river beds was holographically induced. The desert spanned only several miles before ending in a forest of pine trees.

The amount of energy used to generate a force field this size was enormous. David wondered where the generators were housed. Or had Mommy somehow tapped into one of the closed city's power plants? At times he could discern the use of holograms in the wilderness. A tree would turn out to be less tall than it appeared, or a path leading to a clearing visible through the trees would end in a deep ravine. Except for the castle high on the mountaintop, there was no sign of civilization anywhere.

Sometimes he wondered about Irene. How had she been punished? Would he ever see her again?

The nights turned cold and the forest was covered with powdery snow. He slept in caves to keep from freezing, and sucked on ice formed on moss bogs to slake his thirst.

One day Triad returned, walking noiselessly over

the frozen ground. "You must return to the castle now, Master David. You have learned all I can teach you. When the time comes, you will have to be your own teacher."

"I don't want to go back to the castle, Triad," answered David.

"The Lady wants you, Master David. Now is not the time to escape."

David looked up at the tall Black man and knew he was telling the truth. "You should just call me David," he said with a smile, and held out his hand. "I know in my heart you are a friend."

Triad grasped his hand firmly. "Be careful now . . . David." He hesitated as he said the name without the prefix that Mommy had assigned to it. "When you are in the castle, the Lady can hear all you say and watch all you do. She is . . ." but the man stopped himself, leaving David to wonder what control Mommy could possibly have over Triad.

·Nine·

David reached the summit of the mountain and the upper walkway just as the sun was beginning to sink over the horizon in a cloud of blazing red and orange.

The shadows under the arches were black. The ground was cold and hard. The flower beds in the center of the walkway were empty. There was a rustle of silk on the winding stairs. Lady Anastasia walked toward him across the frozen ground. She had wrapped a long fur cape about her. Her flaming red hair danced in the wind.

"Welcome, my little boy blue," she said as she approached. "It was good of you to come back. You learned your lessons well, but winter is coming to the lands below. I am pleased with you, my son."

David flinched. He hoped the darkness would hide the hate he was sure showed on his face. "Of course I came home, Mommy," he said.

The Lady reached out and took his hand. "Come, David, the children are waiting. We have missed you. Go to your room, now, and change for dinner." She led him toward the stone stairs, and together they descended into the castle.

After dinner Mommy announced that a newcomer was to be welcomed in the great hall. David and the rest of the children filed into the stone room to wait. They stood silently in rows with a wide path from the door to Mommy's dais. The Lady was dressed in a ceremonial gown of gold with jewels sewn into the folds of the satin. She had arranged her hair so that it surrounded her face like a red halo.

The huge metal doors were shut. As they silently swung inward, Mommy rose to her feet. The new-

comer, a boy, was struggling wildly as Sarke pro-
pelled him forward.

"I am not fostering this month," yelled the boy.
"There's been a mistake. This is kidnapping!"

As Sarke dragged the screaming boy toward
Mommy, David realized that it was none other than
Willard. Willard Patterson, the boy in his class whom
he had never liked, who had watched him get into
the car with Sarke so long ago. Willard was three years
younger than David. David had always towered over
him. Now they were the same size and apparently
the same age. Willard had grown older, David had
not. Their eyes met.

"That's David Bennet," screamed Willard. "David,
don't you remember me? What have they done to
you? What is this place?"

David looked away. He knew that he could not
risk Willard's recognition of him. Willard began sobbing. "What have they done to you, David?" he cried.

Mommy rubbed her hands impatiently. "Oh, take
him away," she said angrily. "He'll adjust to us in
time. David, come here. The rest of you, go." She
waved her hand imperiously, and the children filed
out of the huge room.

"Yes, Mommy?" David stood before the Lady.

"This Willard, do you know him?" The Lady's eyes
were cold and hard.

David paused before he answered. Mommy knew
everything about everyone who entered the castle.

Of course she knew that he and Willard had gone to the same school. Was this a test? Would she expect the drugs to have wiped out all memory of his former life as it had with Irene? David decided to take a chance. "How could I, Mommy? This was his initiation," he answered calmly.

"He seemed to recognize you."

David shrugged his shoulders. "He was mistaken then. This is my home. You are my mother." He kept his voice level.

The Lady narrowed her lavender eyes into slits. "Your answer is satisfactory, David," she said softly. "But I wonder perhaps you have learned your lessons too well."

David and the Lady stared at each other. "May I return to my chamber now, Mommy?" he asked.

The Lady flicked her hand in a dismissing gesture. Her jewels danced and sparkled. "Yes, yes, of course," she said slowly. David bowed, turned, and left the Great Hall.

Alone in his room, he turned over the unexpected arrival of Willard Patterson to the castle. Was Willard a trap? They had never been friends. Yet Willard could represent a link to the outside world. Perhaps he would know what had happened to David's parents. But how to make contact without being observed?

Tired, David sank onto the bed. He glanced at the soft satin sheets with apprehension. He knew he would be hybed tonight, and he had no way of knowing

for how long. Nevertheless, as long as he pleased
Mommy, she would waken him sometime. He forced
himself to smile as he pulled the covers about him.
He fell almost instantly asleep.

When he did wake up, the sun was streaming in
through the narrow stone windows. David dressed
thoughtfully. How long had he been asleep this time?
he wondered.

At breakfast he saw Willard. He was dressed like
the others in a medieval costume. The color of his
cape was a dusty peach velvet. Willard glanced at
David and averted his eyes. He had apparently learned
some lessons while David slept. David ate his food
quietly, then joked with some of the younger children who loved to snuggle in his lap.

Irene's place was still vacant. But he knew better
than to ask. He prayed she was still alive. He knew
he was to report later in the morning to Sarke for
lessons in weaponry. In the time period remaining he
decided to go up to the upper walkway and think.

As David climbed the twisting stone stairs, he
thought he heard footsteps behind him, but they
stopped whenever he stopped. Had Mommy sent
someone to spy on him? He was so tired of always
watching how he acted and what he said. He missed
the time he had spent in the forest below.

A sharp wind blew across the walkway. Although
there was no snow on the ground, sheets of ice had

frozen over the puddles, and the side of the mountain glistened silver in the bright morning light.

Suddenly David felt a presence beside him. He turned sharply. "Triad!" he gasped.

The dark-skinned man raised his hand in warning. "Now is the time, Master David. Follow me!"

David did not hesitate. He followed Triad across the frozen ground of the walkway gardens.

"We must hurry. This is your only chance," Triad whispered, his scars glistening in the sun. Silently, the two vaulted over the stone wall and landed on a steep ramp that cut back into the mountain.

The quiet was broken by a desperate sob. "David, please wait for me!" It was Willard. "Please let me escape with you!"

Triad scowled. "He will slow us down, David."

"I'll die here!" pleaded Willard.

"You can come," said David sharply. "I'll take responsibility for him," he added to Triad.

They followed Triad across the ramp and into a dark hole in the side of the mountain.

"I have disabled the observation systems here. This is your only chance. But you must be quick. There is a gate in the force field. You almost found it, David. I hoped you would. But you were being observed, and I could not help you. Quickly now!"

They scrambled through the hole, then down a broken iron staircase that plunged over a steep cliff.

Willard panted loudly in the darkness. At the base of
the cliff they ran down another ramp and onto another staircase. This staircase was so broken and frag-
mented that at times they had to cling with their
fingers before dropping several feet to the next stair.
David, for all his training, began to feel his arms and
legs aching. He worried about Willard, whose noisy
breaths crashed through the silence like a pursued
animal. He tried to help him as much as he could.

Finally they reached a level place and entered a
dark hall. Triad ran faster now, and David, hauling
Willard with him, was hard-pressed to keep up with
him.

There was a burst of light. The tunnel opened up
into the forest.

"We've got to rest," panted David.

"There's no time to rest!" answered Triad harshly.

"I don't know if I'm going to make it," gasped
Willard.

"Don't talk," ordered David shortly.

"I have to talk. If we don't make it, I might not
get another chance. David, your father's been searching for you for the last two years. He never gave up.
But there's going to be a war between the Guardians.
I don't think anybody's going to live through it. Your
mom got on the last ship," panted Willard.

"My father stayed?"

Willard nodded, and moaned as he stumbled. David

caught him. "He's looking for you. Most people left. The school closed. The ships got crowded again. But now there aren't any more ships, and I guess we're trapped here. A lot of people are going to die very soon. But I don't want to die in that castle, David. I want to go home."

Suddenly, David's foot caught in a tree root. He lurched forward, dragging Willard with him. Willard screamed. Triad halted. David leapt to his feet and began pulling at Willard.

"I think my leg is broken," moaned Willard. "You'll have to go on without me."

"He speaks correctly, Master David," said Triad. "It will slow us down to take him."

"But I was the one who fell. We can't leave him. How far are we from the gate?" asked David.

"At least another mile."

"Then I'll carry him."

"No," moaned Willard, as David hoisted him on his back.

But David settled Willard's weight against his spine, bent forward, and, holding both of Willard's arms tight, began running again after Triad. The mile seemed to last forever. The ground was uneven, and low hanging branches swatted against his face. Soon his skin was covered by a stinging mixture of blood and sweat.

Finally, Triad pulled up sharply and turned into the trunk of a large tree. It was the gate of Mommy's force field. As David entered the tree, he could see the gate, several yards thick, but very small. They would have to pass in single file. Through the opening, they could see the outlines of a city and a network of unused roads.

"Hurry!" whispered Triad hoarsely.

"Willard first," said David. "He's hurt, and Mommy will surely kill him."

Willard began crawling on his stomach through the gate.

"Yes," shrilled a terrifying voice. "Yes, I will surely kill him, as I will surely kill you!" Lady Anastasia, with Sarke at her side, had appeared.

"I'll bring help! I promise!" shouted Willard, as he rolled clear of the gate.

Triad pushed David behind him as he faced the Lady. "Escape, David," he said.

David backed slowly into the gate. He could hear the outside sounds of the real world. He could see the shimmering of the force field.

At that moment Mommy aimed a hand-held destroyer at Triad. "Join your precious sister," she said as she fired.

Triad staggered back. "All these years I thought she was alive," he gasped. "You lied, Lady."

David darted forward and caught Triad in his arms. The gate melted closed behind him.

Mommy looked scornfully down at the man who

lay dead in David's arms. "Yes, I lied," she said contemptuously and flicked her jeweled skirts clear of
the fallen leaves.

·*Ten*·

David followed Sarke and the Lady back to the castle. A ground car at the base of the mountain took
them back up to the living area.

"If you are wise, Master David, you will say nothing," said Sarke, and smiled at the boy.

"Of course he will say nothing," shrilled the Lady.
"But he has disobeyed. He must be punished. I am
angry with you, David, very angry."

David remained silent. The ground car took them
to Mommy's private chamber, which he had never
seen before. The room was huge, almost as big as the
great hall. Torches burned from stone sockets in the
wall, and everywhere were holograms of the world
and its topography. There were motion charts, whose
purpose David could not decipher, covered with multicolored lines that continuously undulated over a graph
surface.

Through a huge golden arch, David could glimpse

the sleeping area. Mommy's enormous silken mattress rested on the cradle of a huge green-and blue-
patterned crescent that rocked slowly as it spun on an
invisible axis. Above her mattress another crescent
hung, mirroring the moves of the lower one. As David
stared, he realized the arrangement was intended to
represent the planet Earth, with Mommy's bed slic-
ing through the center of it. He thought he could
even see a pattern of silver stars on her ceiling.

"Come, David," said the Lady Anastasia sweetly.
"You have been naughty. Sarke will take you to your
room."

David had no choice. He followed Sarke through
the corridors to his own chamber. The man left him
at his own door. Alone, he paced nervously. He knew
that Mommy would keep him separate from the other
children, at least for a while. He wondered if Willard
had managed to crawl to safety, or if he had somehow
been hunted down and killed before he reached the
authorities. And could the authorities do anything,
even if they knew about Mommy? He also wondered
about what Willard had said. Was the War imminent?
Had the Guardians finally reached some sort of im-
passe out of which the only solution was to end it all?

David heard a knock on the door. Someone had
brought a tray of food and left it. The steam rose and
curled from covered silver dishes. David took the tray
inside, and ate the red meat and steamed grasses sea-
soned with pepper. He had gotten used to the strange

fare of the castle. Then he bathed in the enormous marble tub and put on his silk sleeping attire.

This night, however, he determined *not* to fall a-sleep. The dishes from dinner were still on a tray by his bed. As he moved it beside the window, he secretly cut the skin on one hand and hid a portion of the grass in the fist of the other. Then as he lay in bed, his eyes aching to close, no doubt affected by some chemical released in the air, he rubbed the grass over the cut. It stung and smarted painfully. His eyes stayed open, and though his body felt heavy, he did not surrender to sleep.

After a short time David experienced a sinking feeling. At first he thought it was sleep, then he realized that the bed in his room was slowly descending. He rolled away in time to see it disappear into the floor. Shaking, he backed to the door, but could not even find the handle. He ran to the window, but it was too narrow to climb out. He searched for the light control, but it too had vanished. The room was very dark. He wondered if he were dreaming. Uncertain of what to do, he crept into the armchair and hugged his knees to his chest. He stared at the place where his bed had been. In the gloom it looked like a black puddle in the middle of the floor. The room became stiflingly warm.

Suddenly, the outline of the door became visible. It opened. The room became lighter, just light enough to reveal a figure. Mommy!

"Now you really *have* been naughty, little boy blue,"
she said in her awful voice.

For a moment all David could do was stare at her.
"What are you going to do with me?" he finally asked
in a low voice.

"Get back into bed, my darling, and go to sleep. I
will watch over you. No harm can come to you while
I am here," she said gently. But there was a menacing quality in her voice that was truly frightening.

David turned. The bed was in its usual place, with
the sheets all rumpled as he had left them. "Yes,
Mommy," he said. He backed cautiously to the bed
and lay down, pulling the covers up protectively over
his body.

The Lady Anastasia motioned with her hand. Sarke
appeared in the door and bowed deeply. "I shall stay
with our little David until he falls asleep," she said
imperiously. "Now move the chair close to his bed
so that I can sit next to him."

Sarke nodded, and placed the armchair close to the
head of David's bed. The Lady, with a sweeping gesture that spread her long skirts about her in a practiced swirl, seated herself in it. She waved dismissal
to Sarke. The man bowed, the door shut, and David
was alone with Mommy.

"My poor little boy," she said, as she smoothed
the covers with her white hand. "Perhaps it is my
fault. I have spoiled you. You are my favorite son,

you know. It hurts me to have to punish you. But time is running out, and there are so many lessons to learn. Especially as you are to be the prince. A prince has to be wise in all things. Of all my children, you have scored the highest in intelligence and inherent physical aptitude. But you must learn to obey me. For I am the queen."

"The Guardians," croaked David. The air was thick with a sweet smell, and he could feel his body being dragged into sleep.

"Fear not. I know everything that happens here in my kingdom and out there. I shall protect you. In the end you shall thank me." The Lady began stroking David's forehead. Her hand was cold, and her red nails scratched his skin like thin claws. "Sleep, my little boy, sleep," she crooned.

David could resist no longer. His body and mind surrendered to sleep. But he was vaguely aware that Mommy had stopped stroking his forehead. He felt his bed begin to sink. Then absolute blackness blanketed his thoughts and awareness.

When he opened his eyes, he was in a strange room. The walls were covered in beautiful flowers with long, twisting, green stems. But as he stared, he realized the stems were twisting worms, and the flowers were nothing but multicolored microchips. Suddenly, Mommy's children stood before him. They were

dressed in ceremonial white, but on their heads they
had huge round hats. David realized the hats looked
like little planets.

"They're not hats, we grew them," said Alan in a
shrill voice.

"But you're dead, Mommy killed you," said David,
perplexed.

"Have a piece of my world," answered Alan, and
he broke off a section of the sphere on his head. Underneath, David could see pink flesh exposed. Then
the other children began breaking off sections of their
spheres and eating them. The worms slid off the walls
and began sucking up the pieces that fell to the floor.
David felt the cold pressure of a worm winding up
his leg. He reached up, and felt a huge globe growing
out of the top of his head.

David opened his eyes. The room was dark and quiet.
It was only a dream, he thought to himself. The Lady
was still sitting in the chair. Through the darkness he
could see the outline of her skirts and her strange,
wild hair. But it wasn't the Lady, it was his father.
Jack Bennet came toward the bed. He brushed back
his hair in a nervous gesture. "So you finally woke
up," he said. "We were about to call the medicart.
Had us really worried."

"Dad, I—"

"Darling, darling, our little boy has finally woken
up," called Jack to his wife.

Another form came toward the bed. David smiled up at his mother. It was so good to be home. But it wasn't Mary Bennet who stood over him. It was Mommy. "My favorite boy, my little boy blue," she crooned. "We're so glad to have you back." She rested her hands on Jack Bennet's shoulders. He grinned up at her affectionately. However, when the Lady lifted her hands, David could see red prints on his father's jacket where her fingers had rested. He glanced at the floor. It was wet and shiny. His sheets were spattered with red.

"I'm going to take very good care of you," said Mommy in a little girl voice. She came toward David, and he could see red stains on the tips of her fingers.

"No, no," he cried.

David opened his eyes. He was in the woods. His back hurt because he had been sleeping on a tree root. Triad stood before him. "Come, Master David," he said, and it seemed that his pink scars were slithering all over his face. "It is time to hunt."

"Just call me David," said the boy as he stretched first one arm, then the other. "I keep having nightmares, Triad. I keep thinking I've finally woken up, and I never wake up."

"Well you're awake now, Master David," said Triad kindly. "Come, it's time to hunt. We need food for the winter." Triad stretched out his hand and pulled David to his feet. Together they walked through the

 the air.
Where the pine trees blocked the sun, it was cold,
like ice. They set traps between trees with leather
thongs stretched tight. David practiced his aim as he
threw large round stones at an imaginary target on a
tree trunk.

"Will the quarry come this way?" he asked cheerfully. "I'm getting very hungry."

"Yes, Master David. Here they come now."

David could hear a rustling in the bushes. He hid
quickly behind a tree. It was cold, and the bark
scratched his back. As he glanced out, he could see a
meadow through the trees. It was a bright green, dot-
ted with millions of daisies. The sun was shining
bright. He could hear the sound of laughter. Children
he had never seen before began running noisily into
the wood. They were naked. David was angry. They
would spoil his snares and scare away the animals. He
was very hungry.

"They come now," said Triad in a low voice.

Just behind the children, in the meadow, strode
Mommy. Her red hair was flying wildly in the breeze.
She was laughing. "Run quickly into the forest, my
darlings," she caroled gaily. "Triad has a wonderful
surprise for you. But you must run very quickly."

"They're coming, Master David. Get your stones
ready!"

"Not the children, Triad," gasped David. To his

horror, there was a large smooth white stone in his hand.

"But you are the master," answered Triad simply.

David tried to throw the stone away, but as it flew through the air, it struck the head of a small boy who was singing as he scampered through the leaves. The song stopped. There was a moan as the child sank to his knees. He looked reproachfully at David as his fingers tentatively touched the open wound. Horrified, David stood still where he was. There was another stone in his hand.

"We need meat, David, meat for the winter." This time Triad's voice was stern.

The Lady Anastasia entered the forest. Her gown glowed red. "You are very naughty, David."

"But I—"

"It's your job to provide meat for the castle! You have failed me. Have I spoiled you? Have I spoiled you?" she shrieked. The small boy on the ground looked up fearfully at David and began to sob.

When David opened his eyes, he saw Mommy staring at him. He was tired.

"You see, you can't get away from me, even in your dreams," said the Lady gently.

"Am I still dreaming?" asked David weakly.

"I'll never tell," answered the Lady coquettishly. She reached forward to caress David. He shrank back into the silken sheets. There was something wrong with her hands. Instead of five fingers on each hand, she had at least ten. They wiggled and writhed like little white snakes. "Too many fingers?" she asked. "Sarke will teach you arithmetic." She began breaking off her fingers. When she had gathered three of them in the fist of one hand, she held them out to David. "You see, I always feed my children," she said gently. "I am a good mother." She had stopped laughing. As she leaned toward him, her eyes turned from lavender to red.

David opened his eyes and,
    David opened his eyes and,
        David opened his eyes and,
            David opened his eyes and . . .

· Eleven ·

David opened his eyes and found the room bathed in light. Someone was sitting in the chair by the bed. He shrank back, thinking it was Mommy, and that yet another dream had begun.

"It's okay, David. You can wake up now."

David focused his eyes. It was Irene. He could see

her bright golden hair soft on her shoulders. "The dreams," he muttered. His tongue felt thick in his mouth. His head ached.

"They're over now," said Irene reassuringly. "You must try and get up."

"I feel sick." A wave of nausea hit David as he tried to lift his head. He sank back into the pillow.

"She punishes you with dreams. She keeps you on the edge of sleep with the portable hybernator unit and stimulates some part of your brain with an electronic whip. I've seen it done to others." The girl hesitated. "I've seen children sleep for weeks and scream continuously."

"How long was I—"

"I don't know. I was punished also. It doesn't do any good to talk about it. You'll feel better when your body is stronger."

David staggered out of bed. His legs shook and trembled as he started to stand. He staggered toward the bathroom and splashed a handful of cold water on his face. As he dried himself with the soft, clean towel, he caught sight of his reflection in the mirror. His skin was deathly pale, his eyes were rimmed with black, and the skin on his cheeks was drawn so tight he could practically see the bones underneath.

"What's wrong with me, Irene?" he gasped. He looked at his hands as they trembled. They were so wasted that he could see every vein and muscle.

"The procedure is hard on your body. But you're one of the lucky ones."

"Why?"

"You lived," answered Irene simply.

"Is Mommy still angry with me?"

"No, David. Mommy's very fair. You were punished, and she's forgiven you. She loves you very much."

"You call this love? She nearly killed me! What's wrong with you, Irene?" shouted David angrily. Irene flinched and took a step back. David sighed. It was no use. Irene had lived too long in the castle. "It's all right," he said gently. "I'm not going to hurt you."

"I came to tell you it's time for breakfast," said Irene hesitantly. "I know you don't feel like eating, but you must get your strength back. I'll help you."

David leaned hard on Irene's shoulder. "But I'm still in my sleeping clothes," he joked, trying to get her to smile.

"It doesn't matter. Mommy will treat you as if you've been sick. But please, David, don't say anything about dreams or punishments, it only makes her angry."

David nodded; he knew Irene had not forgiven him for his outburst, but she would in time. When you distorted time, there was no consistency in anything anymore, nothing but the strange laws of the castle that were just whims of Mommy's.

It took David several days to recover his strength.

He knew the time was actually longer, but the deep hybing had its usual recuperative effect. He gained the weight he had lost, and his muscles became firm with exercise. He actually looked forward to the end of each day, knowing that he would sleep deeply and long and without dreams.

There was an air of waiting about the castle. Mommy was nervous. She strode up and down the long halls and muttered to herself. Sarke was nowhere to be seen. Children began disappearing. David knew better than to ask where they were. Then one day the horses disappeared and there was no more riding out in formation. Finally, there were only twelve children left. David was glad that Irene remained. The smaller children roamed the castle in a pack, as if their number gave them safety.

Once, Lady Anastasia grabbed David by the shoulders and shook him. "I haven't taught you all you need to know," she shrilled angrily. "There's no time now." She stared wildly past his head, pushed him away, and continued walking.

David spent a lot of time in the upper walkway. The air was fresh and cold. It was still winter. Down below, the forest carried a thick mantle of white snow. Sometimes Irene joined him. She would curl herself up in a long white cape and nestle beside him. David put his arm around her.

"Is the world going to end?" she asked on the last day.

"I don't know," he answered quietly.

"I hope I'm with you when it does." Irene looked up at him with her soft blue eyes.

David smiled down at her and stroked her hair back from her face. "Yes," he said, and found himself wanting to kiss her, just once.

Instead he rose to his feet. Then he took Irene's hand, and they walked together to the stone ledge.

"I wonder what's going on—out there," said Irene.

"The same thing as here," answered David solemnly. "Everything's falling to pieces." He thought he could even see the outline of the huge force field that surrounded the kingdom begin to crack and shimmer in the cold winter light.

There was the crunch of heavy footsteps on the frozen ground.

"You're to come to the Lady immediately." It was Sarke. He was dressed in black, and his deep voice was loud and threatening. Irene gasped and gripped David's arm.

"Of course, Sarke," she murmured as she backed toward the stone stairs.

"I have to get the others," growled Sarke, pushing past her. "You're to come immediately."

David grabbed Irene's hand. "Quick, Irene, this way," he whispered. He dragged her toward the place Triad had shown him, and pushed Irene over the wall and onto the stone ramp. "This is our chance to escape!" He pulled her down the ramp and into the hole to the hidden staircase.

"Where are we going?" panted Irene.

"We're leaving. We're going outside!" answered David sharply.

"But is there really a world out there?" Irene asked as she ran down the steep stairs.

"Irene, don't you remember? Your parents and the mining accident—friends, a school."

"Sometimes I get confused. There are so many dreams," Irene answered sadly.

They reached the second ramp and then the broken staircase. Sections of it had been hacked off, so that the iron was twisted and bent. In some places it was charred. David peered nervously down through the darkness. Far below, in the gloom, he thought he saw a landing. "We'll have to jump," he said to Irene.

She bent forward and squinted down. "I can't jump that far, David. We'll have to go back. I'll go back."

"No!" David's voice was loud and echoed strangely. "I'll lower you as far as I can. Then you must land light on your feet as Sarke has taught you. There's a platform down there. I can see it."

"All right," said Irene hesitantly. She clutched at David's hands as he lowered her over the edge of the metal precipice. David lay on his stomach and inched forward so that Irene would have less of a fall.

"I see the platform, David," she whispered. "You can drop me now. I'll be all right."

David's fingers were wrapped tight about the slender wrists. All of a sudden he realized that he didn't want to drop Irene onto the platform. Something was wrong. He could feel it.

"No," he muttered. "I'm pulling you back up."

"It's all right, David," called Irene.

David felt his grip begin to weaken. He tried to tighten his fingers, but her hands slipped away. He reached down wildly. He saw Irene fall. She screamed.

David squinted into the darkness. A figure was holding Irene. Sarke! Irene looked up at David. Her face was round and white.

"David!" she cried.

"Bring the girl, Sarke," shrilled a familiar voice behind David. "I'll tend to the boy."

David struggled to his feet. "Don't punish Irene, Mommy, please!" he begged.

"There's no time for punishments, you fool! There's no time at all!" The Lady grabbed David's arm and pulled him back up the ramp. She began running, and her nails dug into his skin as she dragged him along.

Halfway up the ramp, she turned into an archway. After several twists of the corridor, David realized they were in a familiar part of the castle. The gong that divided the day into time portions reverberated continuously. The lights flickered on and off. The holograms in the walls pulsated.

Lady Anastasia pulled David through her chamber. He glimpsed her huge bed, formed in the center of a model Earth, now spinning erratically. There was a door, then a vacuum lift sucked them down into the depths of the mountain. David was pushed into a small, windowless room. The lights here burned fiercely bright.

"Irene!" screamed David.

"Sarke will prepare her," said Lady Anastasia triumphantly. "And now for the Prince!"

David backed away. "No," he gasped.

"You fool. The world is ending. You will sleep until the danger is passed. When you wake, you will conquer the world with my army of children. You will be their leader. I have chosen you. All around you in stone chambers the children sleep. And when they wake, I will teach you how to lead them to victory. I am the mother of the new race!"

Mommy pointed a destroyer at David's chest until he stepped slowly backward.

As he lay on the flat metal table in the center of the room, the sides began to rise around him. He could hear the Lady moving about the room. The walls began to close over him.

"And now to seal this room safe from Sarke," he heard Lady Anastasia say. "My little Prince will sleep a long time. I will guard him. No one will ever find him, except for me, when the time is right and the world is new again."

· *Twelve* ·

"Dr. Bennet, Dr. Bennet, please let me in! It's about David."

Jack rubbed his eyes. He had been staring at the monitor for so long that he feared he might have slipped into sleep. There was a strong wind blowing outside, and the door was rattling violently.

"Dr. Bennet!" came the agonized voice.

Jack touched the entrance button on the console, and immediately the front door swung open. A boy stood there, one of David's friends at school. But he had been missing for months. "Come in . . ."

The youth rushed in. His clothes were torn, and there was a wild look in his eyes. "I'm Willard, Willard Patterson. Dr. Bennet, I . . . I've seen David. He's alive. But he's a prisoner. That Lady Anastasia has all these children, I mean hundreds of children. She's saving them."

Jack ran his hand over his forehead. For a moment all he could think of was David's alive. My son is alive! He stared at Willard, unable to understand what he was saying.

"She's deep-hybing them."

"That's not possible," snapped Dr. Bennet. He now wondered if perhaps the Patterson boy had lost his mind. Insanity levels were on the rise as the War approached. "There are no hybe units in the private sector. It's against the law."

"The law? Dr. Bennet, Lady Anastasia has her own kingdom, force fields around it. David's the same age as he was when he disappeared. She makes her own laws, and Sarke carries them out."

"Sarke?" asked Jack. All his research on Joshua Sarkoman came flooding to the surface of his mind.

"He's her servant, or something. He enjoys hurting people. They both do. We've got to get David out of there."

"Have you told anyone else?" asked Jack.

"No." Willard's voice began to shake. "I got home somehow. But I don't know where my parents are. My leg was broken. I fell while we were trying to escape. David carried me. He could have left me, but he didn't.

"I tried to contact law enforcement on my monitor, but the line was down. I tried to contact you, but all I got was a message that said all communications were temporarily discontinued. I couldn't even get a medicart link-up. Finally, a transient robo-med set my leg."

"How did you get here?" asked Jack.

"My bike. I know it sounds crazy. I was studying antique forms of transportation last term, before the schools closed, and I learned how to ride it. I remembered how to get here, because I always look out the windows when our car takes us places."

"You rode on a bicycle, with wheels?" asked Jack incredulously. For a moment his astonishment blocked out all other thoughts. Willard nodded.

"I want to believe you, Willard. I want to believe that David is still alive."

"You have to! He saved me! If it wasn't for David, I'd still be there. God knows how he's been punished."

"Let's go," said Jack quickly. Punishing my son? he thought in outrage to himself. And then he felt a wave of pride as he realized that David had sacrificed his freedom for another. But it was Willard that stood before him, not David. Why couldn't it be David? Why?

As they drove along, he lapsed into a daydream. It was a familiar one that he had been having often. He saw David before him, and David reached out his hands and said, "Hi, Dad. I'm home." Then Mary would come running, with her hair all blowing and tangled. "I took a shuttle craft back. I couldn't go into hybe without you." And she laughed, and they all laughed together, and the sun was warm on their faces. Sometimes Mary was holding the baby, and it looked just like David when he was born.

It was a four-hour drive to the force field. Although the entire sector was closed, the computer check at the barrier had ceased functioning. Jack's spirits rose higher and higher.

Finally they could see the glimmer of a protective field. It seemed huge, spanning the horizon with a glistening mist. Jack drove his car straight up to it. He got out and tried to push his hand through. He felt the familiar tingling of an active field followed by stonelike resistance as the molecules rearranged themselves.

It seemed he walked and drove for miles and still the force field continued.

"David's in there," Willard kept saying.

But in the end Jack had to give up. The force field was impenetrable. Through it he could see the distant outline of a mountain, tall and menacing against the horizon.

"I'll come back with more people," Jack said firmly. "I'll get my son out somehow."

The return trip was silent. Willard slept most of the way. Jack put the car on autopilot, but tired as he was, he couldn't sleep. To get so near to David and yet fail. It seemed as if his daydream had vanished forever.

But he still had the project. He thought briefly of Sharon Weisman, and wondered if she had made any progress. She was unreachable, of course. But how she would have approved of what he was doing.

It was the people who made it so important, the ones who had been left behind. They were so eager to help and learn. Already the shelter had been dug two miles deep using an abandoned mining shaft as a base. Food was beginning to be smuggled in. Construction of air filters and oxygen producers had started. And it was all without the knowledge of the Central Computer. There was almost a sense of euphoria among the people.

But if they did manage to survive the destruction, what kind of world would be left? Insects, grass, and radiation. The people would have to stay underground for many years until the air cleared. And even then, the radiation would probably reach them through tiny cracks in the earth, causing genetic mutations that would only be amplified by the inevitable inbreeding. He had tried to contact the Survivalists to include them in the project, but they had hidden themselves somewhere and were unreachable. How many other groups of people are there on this continent, around the world, all doing the same thing, trying to figure out a way to survive? he wondered.

He was so lonely without Mary. Always she had been there for him to talk to. It made his ideas clearer. He glanced at Willard, his head tipped back and his mouth open. He reminded him a bit of David. Poor boy, he'd obviously been through a lot, and his leg had been badly set by the robo-med, probably an earlier model. Where were Willard's parents?

There were so many people who had just gotten in their cars and begun driving, in some insane hope that they could reach a deserted-enough spot where the missiles wouldn't strike. They would all die slowly or quickly from the radiation. Life aboveground did not have a chance.

"Insects and grass," he murmured to himself sadly. "Insects and grass."

"What, Dr. Bennet?" asked Willard, opening his eyes.

"Nothing, Willard. But I was thinking, would you like to help me? I'm trying to organize a group of people to live underground through the War. It will be a long time before we can come to the surface of the Earth again, and it won't be easy."

"You'd take me?" asked Willard incredulously. "Of course. I'll do anything."

"You've already done more for me than any other person. I know that my David is alive." Jack ran the back of his hand over his eyes quickly. "Now, Willard, we have an important project to do. We will have to gain access to the research laboratory and smuggle out two rabbits, more if we can."

"Rabbits?"

"Yes, to live underground with us until it's safe to come out."

Willard took a breath. "Why?" he asked cautiously.

Jack nodded. He expected this reaction. It was so

hard to get people to understand that saving themselves meant saving other things as well. "After the
war, when the radiation has cleared and it is safe to
come out, we will be faced with a world of insects
and grass," he explained slowly. "Everything else will
have been destroyed—trees, animals, crops. Our rabbits will be able to survive just by eating the grass.
They will provide food and clothing for us. They will
be the perfect domestic animal—small, disease-resis-
tant, and with the ability to multiply quickly. You
see, it's not enough just to save whatever people we
can. We have to somehow make that future world
livable for them."

Willard looked down at the floor. When he spoke,
Jack could barely hear him. "Dr. Bennet, what's it
going to be like . . . then?"

"I'm an anthropologist, not a fortune-teller. I've
spent my whole life studying the development of the
human race. What's it going to be like? There will
be nothing left, Willard. No technology, no tools, no
shelter. The knowledge of what we have accom-
plished so far—electricity, space travel, scientific laws,
even metals and plastics—will fade, and survive only
in myths. It will be back to square one for the human
race. At least my people will have an edge against
that. It took millions and millions of years for primitive man to reach the point where he raised animals
for food and cultivated crops. I will leave for my people laws to live by and a type of domestic animal that

will flourish in the hostile environment of the time after the destruction."

Jack felt a surge of energy as he talked. Willard Patterson had brought him at least the assurance that David was alive. And just having someone to talk to made his thoughts and his goals so much clearer. There was so much to do, and so little time. And above all, he had to reach David before the destruction came.

· *Thirteen* ·

David heard the click of the door closing. Then there was a dull rumble that increased in volume until it became deafening. The metal walls folded completely over him, and he saw and heard no more.

Irene struggled wildly in Sarke's grasp. Above her, she could dimly see the pale outline of David's face as he peered down at her. "David!" she screamed. "David!" Then Sarke covered her mouth with his hand and yanked her down a dark corridor that she had never seen before. "Where are you taking me?" she demanded.

Sarke laughed. "Anastasia was right," he said. "All these years I thought she was crazy."

"Where are you taking me?" Irene tried to pull her arm away from Sarke, but he twisted it cruelly, until she leaned into him.

"To sleep, my little princess, for a long long time. And when you wake . . ."

Irene shivered as she heard the leering quality in Sarke's voice. She had known for some time that it was dangerous to be alone with Sarke. "You don't know Mommy's plans for me," she said shrilly. "And she would punish you for talking to me like this."

Sarke knotted his fingers in her hair and forced her head back. Then he traced his finger from her cheek down to the hollow of her neck. She tried not to flinch, but his touch was cold and terrifying.

"Like a little virgin priestess guarding her precious secrets from the world. But when Mommy is dead, who will guard you? I do not think it will be that fair-haired boy who follows you with his eyes."

"Mommy has plans. She knew the world would end," said Irene desperately. "She knew there would be a war."

Sarke turned into one of the main corridors, and now Irene felt her heart begin to pound as she approached what she knew was her hybernation chamber. "Hundreds of years," she kept thinking over and over again. "What if I never wake up?" Always before, there had been Mommy. She had never actually known when she was in hybernation—only that seasons had an odd way of passing quickly, two days of drought-like summer, and the next morning, snow over the mountain. Although she had guessed of its existence, she had never before seen her hybe chamber. Deep hybernation occurred only at night, after she had fallen asleep in her soft, silken bed. And each morning she had woken in the same bed, sometimes with the sound of birds chirping outside the window, and sometimes with Mommy sitting silently in the chair by her bed.

Finally, they stood at the door of a small room. Unlike the rest of the castle, it was square and modern. There were no windows. In the center, on a raised stone platform, lay a simple transparent cylinder with a lacework of tiny wires and glistening sparks patterning the surface. All around, the air thrummed from the self-contained fusion generator.

"It's so ugly," whispered Irene. She thought of the silk gowns, the torchlit processions, the testing, the punishments, and above all, the mystical rites that Mommy had taught her, and *this* was where she would sleep for a hundred years?

Sarke shrugged his shoulders. "It works," he murmured, as if reading her thoughts. "I watched you many times while you lay contained in hybe. So pretty, and you never knew I was watching you."

Irene tried to pull away from Sarke. "Where's Mommy?" she asked, trying to keep her voice from trembling.

"Busy with David, I imagine, my little princess."

"I am not your princess," snapped Irene.

Sarke let the door shut behind him. There was a soft hiss as the room sealed itself, and Irene knew it was useless to try and escape back down the corridor. The room was now virtually without a door. Only Mommy could gain entrance from outside. She backed away from the leering man and tried to put the hybe unit between them.

Sarke laughed. Even when he stopped laughing, his face still wore a malicious grin. "I'm not going to touch you now, Irene," he said in a menacingly soft tone. "For two reasons, my little princess. First, in a few minutes, you must go to sleep. What I have in mind will take a lot longer, hours perhaps, or days . . . an eternity."

"How dare you talk to me like that!" said Irene defiantly. "I would never let you touch me. Mommy would kill you."

Sarke laughed again. "I can be patient, my sweet thing. I can be patient for a hundred years. For I too will sleep. But there's a difference between us. When I wake, I will remember all that has passed. But you, poor innocent, will have forgotten. Deep hybernation does that sometimes. The controls have to be set very precisely, and sometimes I am not very precise." Sarke shrugged his shoulders apologetically, but his eyes were mocking. "When you wake, you will gladly come to my arms. In fact, you will believe everything I tell you. You will love me. No, more than that, Irene, I will make you worship me with your very soul. But don't worry, my dear, I will be a kind master."

"What's this talk of kindness?" Mommy stood in the door. Irene rushed to the security of her embrace. "There, there, my little girl. I know you are frightened. But now you must sleep until the Earth is pure again."

"Please, Mommy, it's not that," gasped Irene. But already, Mommy had disentangled herself from her frightened hold.

"Sarke, is the unit ready?" asked Lady Anastasia briskly. The man nodded. "Now, my little darling, you must lie down in the unit. Just pretend it's like going to sleep."

"What about my secrets?" asked Irene, desperately stalling for time. She couldn't help wondering if David had escaped. Perhaps he could find her. Perhaps even now he was looking for her. But if he hadn't escaped, he too was in great danger. I've got to warn him somehow, thought Irene to herself.

"Have no fear for your precious secrets." Mommy's voice was soothing. "Your mission is indeed a sacred one, my darling. I will see that all is tended to."

"Where's David?"

"Taken care of, my precious child."

Irene felt her heart sink. She struggled to keep the tears from sliding down her face. She knew Sarke was looking at her, gloating and sure of himself. "What about you, Mommy? Will you be here when I wake?"

Mommy smiled gently. "Of course, my darling. Mommy will be right here."

Irene shot Sarke a defiant look as she obediently climbed into the hybe casket. Sarke moved swiftly across the room to adjust the dials. Mommy had already turned away.

"She will be dead," whispered Sarke. "In fact, I will enjoy killing her, almost as much as I will enjoy . . . you."

"Mommy!" screamed Irene. "Mommy!" But already the unit was closing around her, and her voice was deadened. "Please don't let me forget," she whispered silently.

Then the tears began sliding down her cheeks in tiny streams, but because her arms were held against her sides in the darkness, she could not even wipe them away. If there had been a mother before Mommy, the memory was faint. It was Mommy who had held her and comforted her, and cared for her when she was sick. And the punishments, the cruelties, were only because Mommy loved her so much, loved all of them so much. Mommy had promised that she would be there when they woke up, to guide them through the new world. But sometimes Mommy lied. Sometimes she promised things that didn't happen. What if Sarke killed her? Irene began to feel a cold numbness creeping up her legs and arms. When she woke, would Mommy be dead? Sarke leaning over her with a hungry look in his cold eyes? She knew there was only a second or so left before she lost all feeling and thoughts. In her mind she saw Sarke's leering grin taunting her. She tried to clench her fists, but there was no feeling in her hands. *David*, a small part of her mind whispered. Then she slipped down into darkness.

· *Fourteen* ·

Jack leaned back against the cold metal wall of the shelter. He was so tired. Every muscle ached. The overcrowding was draining the facility. There was no place to be alone. And they all kept looking to him for answers.

His hand throbbed. The compu-write devices had given out in the first year. He wrote by hand now. Already it seemed that their tiny underground society was slipping into a primitive existence. "I must outline a fair and democratic government that will work for these people, that they can understand, so that they will never again turn to the outside for decisions," he wrote carefully. His notebooks had become a combination of diary and suggestions for survival. Unfortunately, the seeds he had wanted to save had been contaminated by nuclear radiation. The Earth would be a barren place indeed, and the people would have to rely on whatever grass forms had managed to withstand the radiation bombardment.

He smiled. At least the rabbits were thriving. They were his pet project. They ate the green stone algae in the far caves and were reproducing at a great rate, already supplementing the dwindling food supplies. And Willard had grown into a strong young man. When the time came to leave the shelter, he would be a good leader.

The familiar tightness came again at Jack's chest. He rubbed his hand over the ache. He knew he would not live to step out into the sun again. But David. He had tried so hard to break through the force field. Was David still alive?

He covered his face with his hands. "Oh, Mary," he whispered. "I failed." The old daydream from the Time-Before floated before his eyes. Mary was young, her hair blowing. The sun was shining, and David was with them, tall and blond and laughing in the light.

·*Fifteen*·

"I am David. I am—" But that was all. It was as if
something had been ripped from him, leaving a gap-
ing hole in his brain.

He was standing on a flat, open space under a gray
sky. It was surrounded by stone arches, many of them
crumbled, and a wall that had broken through in several places. An area that might once have held a garden was a barren wasteland of rubble and dust. A
cold wind whistled through the stones. Someone had
led him here, up broken twisted stairs. There was
pain inside his head, blinding, searing pain. "I know
this place," he tried to say, but his lips felt thick and
fuzzy. He looked out over the ledge. The thought,
Where is the forest? formed slowly in his consciousness. In its place there was nothing but undulating
grass, yellow and gray grass blowing in the wind.

There was an evil feeling here. He knew he had
to escape. He had to climb down the mountain and
find . . . But the thought stayed unfinished.

The mountain had changed. In some places it was
smooth as glass. In others it had crumbled in on it-

self. Several times he slipped. By the time he reached the bottom, his hands were scraped.

Night came. He found himself looking up at the black sky for star patterns he could recognize, but found none. He listened for the sound of night birds or small animals that might serve as food, but heard nothing but the creak and snick of insects in the shifting grass. He lit a small fire by smashing his dagger against a stone and catching the sparks in a nest of shredded grass. Someone had taught him these things. He remembered pink scars glistening on black skin. But try as he might for further memories, that was all. As he drifted into sleep, images that he didn't understand floated across his brain.

He woke, shivering with cold. Soon it would be winter. I must get away from the mountain, he thought. In his mind he saw a tall woman with white skin and billowing red hair, and many children all staring at him with round empty eyes.

There was no path through the tall grass. Sometimes the grass grew around huge boulders. Sometimes there were great spaces where nothing grew. A few of the grass stalks still had seed cases clinging to them. He tried chewing the grains. They were dry and tasteless and did little to quell his hunger. He stumbled frequently now. Clouds of biting insects landed on his face and arms, leaving red, itchy bumps and ridges where they had drawn blood.

"Am I in a dream?" he mumbled to himself. "Is

that why I don't know who I am? Why can't I wake up? Why is everything so strange?" A little flicker of memory darted through his brain—a girl with yellow hair who wore a long rose-colored skirt. "She punishes you with dreams," says the girl.

"What did I do?" he asks. But the girl disappears into black.

He walked for three days. The landscape never changed. Tall, reedy grass rustled and shifted in the breeze. Fallen boulders lay half-submerged in the dust. The wind blew constantly.

On the fourth day the grass became shorter and finer. Hunger made him feel faint. The sun was still high in the sky, but he knew he could go no farther. He lay down on the shorter grass and relaxed into sleep.

Suddenly he heard a rustle quite near him, and then another movement in the grass. It was a large movement, too big to be an insect. There was more movement, heavy movement. He opened his eyes to find himself surrounded by huge brown rabbits, the size of small goats. Apart from their size, their eyes were disproportionately small, and set far back on their heads, under their long furry ears. There were now about twenty of them, all crunching and tearing at the grass. One of the animals sniffed his leg and nibbled at his cloak.

"Hey, stop that," he began to say, as he sat up. But at that moment there was a growl behind him, and something grabbed his shoulder. David turned quickly and gasped in horror. A figure was standing over him. It appeared to be human in that it had two arms and two legs and was wrapped in some sort of fur clothing. But the face . . . the face was distorted and mutilated. The eyes were misplaced, and the mouth appeared to have four lips instead of two. The thing growled angrily at him, and David cowered in horror. It's going to kill me, he thought. It's going to kill me!

· *Sixteen* ·

At first there was nothing. Then the darkness became so heavy that it pressed into her eyes like knotted fists. The cold wrapped around her like a shroud. Someone stroked her hands, then her face. The touch was warm, and the darkness began to lift a little. There was a name, a word that she tried to remember, or was it a fear of something? She began to hear sounds, the sounds of someone near her, silk rustling, and voices.

Finally her eyelids opened but the darkness remained. She tried to move her fingers, but her hands were clenched tight. Now there was mist around her, and through the mist she could see a form bending over her. "Where am I?" she managed to whisper.

"Safe, my princess," was the soft reply.

She struggled to sit up, but the mists pushed her down. Another question was slowly forming. "Who am I?" she asked. The tall man, dressed in black, laughed gently. She wondered why a laugh should frighten her, but somehow she knew that she should not show her fear, so she simply looked at the man.

"You, my dear, are the princess Irene of the new world, soon to be my queen. When you are rested," he said this somewhat sarcastically, "you will meet your subjects."

"What's your name?" asked Irene. It was a profound relief to remember that indeed she was Irene.

The man smiled. "They call me the Black Regent. Soon I will be king. But you, my dear, may call me Sarke. After all, you are my bride."

Irene frowned. There was a wrongness here. But her mind seemed so empty that she knew that for the time being, she would have to rely on this . . . Sarke. He lifted her gently from where she had been lying. His arms were warm, and somehow she felt safe being carried like a child. It was comforting. Perhaps it was not wrong after all to rest her head against his chest and let him care for her.

"Tend the princess," she heard him say. And others lifted her, and bathed her with warm, scented water, and clothed her with soft, flowing silk. When she could walk, they escorted her down a long hall. The mist was still before her eyes, but the attendants led her gently so that she would not stumble.

Finally, she stood alone on a huge platform, her white silk gown swirling out behind her. There were torches burning on the walls. As her sight became clearer, she saw a huge room full of people staring at her. For a moment she wondered if she was supposed to say something, or perform some rite that she had forgotten. To her relief, Sarke came quickly to her side and took her hand in his. "I have awakened Irene," he said in a solemn voice. "And in the name of the sleeping prince, I will wed her when the moon is full. Let a feast be prepared, for in two weeks time, in the name of the sleeping prince, I will claim the kingdom."

A great shout of joy went up from the room. Irene wondered why they worshiped him so much. After all, he . . . but at that moment Sarke raised her hand to his lips, and Irene found herself smiling graciously because she knew . . . that was what Sarke wanted from her.

·Seventeen·

With a snarl, the creature/man lunged at David but did not strike him. Instead he jerked him to his feet and began yanking him through the taller grasses. The rabbits, if indeed they were rabbits, trailed along slowly, every now and then pausing to rip and nibble at the brush.

As they rounded a bend, David saw a cluster of ten or twelve huts fashioned out of reeds. A group of several children ran toward him. Like the man, their features were odd and misshapen. Some limped and others had twisted limbs. They gazed in awe at the newcomer.

He was thrown into a small hut. It was night when they came for him. A fire had been built, and the light made strange shadows on the twisted faces. The man/creature who captured him growled, "Stealing the herd!"

A tall one, who seemed less deformed than the others, stood up. "Are you one of the Children?" he asked.

"Who?"

"The Children, the Children who follow the Black Regent."

There was something about the way the man spoke these words that filled David with dread. "No," he answered, "No, I'm not."

"He's a spy," an old woman croaked. "Kill him!"

"We are the Demosee." The tall man spoke firmly. "The boy must have a fair trial."

"Are they fair when they raid our village? When they steal our children and our herd? Four times this year we have had to move the village to escape. He is formed like them. He is dressed like them. Kill him!" The crowd murmured in agreement.

But the tall man held up his hand. "Where were you going when our Toom found you?" he asked in a quiet voice.

David rubbed his head nervously, as if trying to push away the darkness that covered his brain. "I don't remember . . ." he stammered. "I have to find . . ." There was another spark inside his head as a memory fell into place. "I have to find my father!" he shouted triumphantly.

The people gave an excited gasp and began muttering to each other. Again the tall man held up his hand, and they became silent. "Are you Dahben, son of Jahben?" he asked.

"No. I am David. My father is—I don't remember his name."

The crowd gave a moan of disappointment.

"There is no such person as Dahben!" snarled the old woman. "Spy or not, we don't need an extra mouth to feed."

The tall man shook his head. "He is lost and hungry. And it is clear he has a sickness of the mind. He shall live with us until he remembers who he is. Perhaps there is another village on the other side of the mountain. I think Jahben would want us to care for him. Remember, Jahben wrote, innocent until proven guilty. We must follow the teachings of Jahben, or we will not be worthy of his son."

"Come to us, Dahben, through the darkness. Wake Dahben, to lead the way," chanted the people in unison. Then of one accord, they scattered.

David and the tall man were left standing before the fire alone. "I am Willod," the man said. "I lead the village. It will be safer if you stay with me."

David looked around the small hut to which Willod had led him. There were no windows. In the center was a small ring of stones blackened by many fires. He found himself wondering if he had gone crazy and this strange world was nothing more than a nightmare from which he would wake, but to what? What would he wake up to? There were so many questions. "Who are these children you spoke of?" he asked Willod.

The man looked at him with surprise. "Your sickness must be very deep if you do not know what the Children of Time are," he answered. "They came out of the mountain ten years ago. They were young

then, just children—some only seven years old, but
perfectly formed as you are. We called them the
Children, the Children of Time. You see, we believed that like Jahben, they came from the Time-
Before. But even then they did not act as children.
They hunted us for sport, always following the Black
Regent, their leader. They have huge beasts they call
horses. We think they take the bones of our rabbits
and weave them together with spells and human hair
to make monsters. Perhaps it is fear of them that made
your mind sick. They live inside the mountain, waiting and searching for their Sleeping Prince, their true
leader, who will lead them to conquer the world.
These are evil times. Perhaps the world is ending
and Dahben will never wake." Willod shook his head
sadly. Then he straightened himself. "But we have
the sacred writings of Jahben," he added.

"What do these sacred writings say?" asked David.

"They talk of the Time-Before, and how our people survived the great destruction. How the leaders
flew into the star mantle that covers us at night, taking their knowledge with them.

"Jahben stayed to save our people. My great-
grandfather was a friend of Jahben. I am called Willod, as he was. Jahben gathered the people who were
left and led them underground. The roads to the stars
were closed, and Jahben knew everything aboveground would be killed. All the while he searched for
his son, Dahben, who had been stolen from him. Then

my great-grandfather Willod came with a strange tale. Willod was only a boy, about your age. He spoke of a strange kingdom within the mountain and many sleeping children. Jahben tried to reach his son, but the destruction came."

"What happened to Jahben?" asked David, trembling, as an unexplainable feeling of loss and fear swept over him.

"He did not live to see the sun of the Time-After. But it is he who gave us our herd and the vote by which we decide what is right for the people. And he gave us the sacred writings to guide us in the Time-After. One day his son, Dahben, will come to us and lead us. That is why we wait by the mountain." Willod became silent and stared out at the black night.

David woke to the sun streaming in through the opening in the skin-covered roof of the hut. For a moment he forgot where he was. Willod was stirring something by the fire. The hut was rich with food smells. Willod handed David a clay dish heaped with roasted nuts, cheese, and boiled grains. The nuts were crunchy and heavily salted, but the cheese was rich and sweet.

Because Toom had been the one to find David, David was handed over to the twisted man for instruction in caring for the herd. "I don't want him," growled Toom to Willod.

"You are old, Toom," Willod said gently. "You need someone to help you with the herd."

Toom shook his head stubbornly and glared at the ground.

"David will help you, Toom." Willod's tone was even quieter this time, and it was clear that Toom had no choice.

The largest of the milk rabbits lay on her side while Toom gently tugged at the pink teats that poked through the fur of her stomach. He collected the milk in a leather flask. Trying to help, David patted the rabbit behind her ears. She flinched and snapped at the air.

"Let her smell you first," muttered Toom angrily. "Everyone knows rabbits are blind."

I didn't, thought David to himself. I don't seem to know anything. A surge of unhappiness welled up inside him.

In the days that followed, David learned much about the village. It was a hard life. Yet the people, if they could be called that, helped each other as best they could. And the young were taught to read and write. At first David could not understand the reason for this, as there were no books and the sacred writings of Jahben were for the exclusive use of the leader. But Willod explained that one of Jahben's laws stated that all the village's decisions and discoveries had to be written down and passed from generation to generation. Any one of the children could be a future leader. It was vital for each of them to know how to read and write.

David learned to guide the blind herd through the grass and how to remove the biting insects from their skins that made them itch and tear at their fur with their strong clawed hind feet.

The air turned colder. The herd bunched together for warmth as they crunched at the dry, reedy stems.

"We must work to gather food for the winter," said Toom as he stroked his favorite milk rabbit, who had just delivered a fine litter of six. Five of them would be slaughtered in a month, and the meat dried and salted for winter use. Only the largest female of the litter would be saved.

"In Jahben's time the rabbits were tiny animals. But we bred them larger and larger so that they would give us more meat," explained Willod.

David hated the slaughtering, and he suspected that Toom felt the same. When it was time to slaughter an animal, Toom became moody and sharp-tempered. He would stroke the rabbit gently and croon softly to it. "Has to be done," he would mutter. "But kindly and quickly. Not like them."

David knew he meant the Children of Time, and shivered. His dreams were filled with people he could not remember. There was a boy named Paul and a building called school, with wide empty steps and long halls. In every dream there was a girl with long blond hair, although often he could not see her face. "I'll take you to a Hellions game when you get back," a tall man with gray hair said. Almost every night David woke in the familiar darkness of the hut, with his face wet with tears.

Although the mountain was barely visible on the horizon, its presence seemed to dominate the village. Each day there was always the question: Will Dahben come to us today? How will we know him? Can he find the village through the reeds? And yet there was always the fear of the Children coming from the mountain with their killing and cruelty. And what about their Sleeping Prince, whom the Children searched for by digging in the mountain? They would not leave the mountain until they found him.

And who will come first, David wondered. The Prince, or Dahben?

· *Eighteen* ·

After her presentation to the Children, Irene was escorted to an ornate chamber. The guards who attended her withdrew silently, but when she tried to leave the room, they came to the door and stood before her.

"Ah, my sweet, sweet Irene," said a familiar voice.

"Sarke," answered Irene, and she smiled. It was

reassuring to know someone's name. It helped fill the white void inside her.

He reached over and stroked her cheek with his hand. She found herself pulling back. Sarke's eyes became cold and menacing. "I felt I couldn't breathe," she explained. What she did not say was that she had suddenly felt that his huge hand was smothering her.

"I won't rush you, my precious girl," said Sarke gently. He took her hand and slumped into one of the carved chairs. Then he held her on his lap like a small child. Irene felt safe again and leaned her head against the rich brocade of his cloak.

Food and drink were brought. Sarke did not eat, but encouraged Irene to have her fill. Sometimes he even picked up morsels of meat from the plate and fed her with his fingers. The food was spicy and the water had a metallic taste. "That's a good girl," crooned Sarke as he stroked her head and urged more of the meat to her mouth.

Irene began to feel dizzy. The room was spinning and rocking. It seemed that Sarke had several faces, all staring at her hungrily. She tried to pull away from him, but to her astonishment, when she stood up her legs gave way beneath her and she crumpled to the floor. Sarke slid his arms under her and carried her easily to the bed. Irene found herself clinging to him as if he could stop the spinning of the room. He laid her down and straightened her silken skirts about her.

For a moment he said nothing, then he bent over her and whispered with an eerie intensity, "Tell me, Irene, where are the secrets?"

Irene stared back, uncomprehending. "What secrets?" she asked.

"Don't deceive me," he said sharply. "You were conditioned not to forget the secrets."

Irene felt frightened. "Please, I don't know what you're talking about," said Irene. Why was this man suddenly angry at her? What had she done?

Sarke stared hard at her. Then he traced his finger on her lips. "You will tell me, Irene," he said gently. "Because you will do everything I say. Why already I have you eating out of my hand!" He burst into a loud laugh and pushed his way through the guards. Irene could hear his laughter echoing down the corridors as he strode away.

Sleep came suddenly, almost violently. Irene had the flicker of a thought—I have been drugged!—before the darkness came.

But with the sleep came a peculiar dream. The chamber was dark, except for a thin shaft of moonlight gleaming on the cold stone floor. There was a hunched figure beside her, bending over her, whispering her name. There was a stench of dirt and filth and rotting cloth. "You must not tell him," said the voice urgently.

Irene tried to answer, but could not move her mouth.

"He is trying to control you, like the others. But you *will* resist him. Mommy will help you."

"Mommy?" Irene tried to whisper. An odd feeling of relief and fear washed over her, as numerous images of a tall woman with red hair and lavender eyes flickered in her mind.

"Listen carefully. Under your bed you will find a pitcher of clean water and some food. Every morning it will be there. Do not touch what Sarke gives you." The figure bent over Irene, closer and closer until she closed her eyes.

Suddenly there was a sound in the corridor of footsteps and clanking metal. When Irene opened her eyes again, the room was empty. She stared at the thin shaft of moonlight until her eyes sank slowly shut.

Dawn came. The room was cold and lit by a flat gray light that came from the small window. Irene felt sick. Her head ached. When she tried to stand, the muscles in her legs twitched uncontrollably. Weakly she moved about the room. The handle on the door would not turn. She listened for sounds in the corridor, but everything was quiet. There was a spicy smell in the air.

An elaborate meal had been set for her. There was a golden goblet filled with pale wine, red slivers of meat in a dark sauce, and a flat cake. Her stomach had begun to cramp. She wondered if she were hungry, or sick. Her fingers reached for the cake. It was warm and crumbly. She sat back on the bed holding it. There was something she had to remember, something very important.

"I am Irene," she said softly. She tried to summon up images that would tell her more. She remembered Sarke holding her in his lap and the way her hands clung to him. She shivered. It was an unpleasant memory. There must be something more . . . if only.

"I am in danger," she thought suddenly. It was as if the darkness in her mind lifted for a moment, before gathering again. "Sarke is not my friend. He is my enemy!"

Her dream came back in bits and pieces. She began to feel hungry. Her fingers rolled the bread into grainy bits of dough. She was thirsty also. Her mouth felt fuzzy and tasted bitter. She brought the cake to her mouth. Like the meat, it had a rich, spicy smell. She wondered if indeed it was drugged. But why would Sarke drug her? She replaced the cake and felt under her bed. Her hand brushed against something cold. Carefully she drew it out. It was a simple flask filled with water, and beside it, a chunk of stale bread.

It wasn't a dream! thought Irene to herself. Furtively she drank the water and nibbled at the bread. Every second that passed, she expected a guard or Sarke to enter her chamber. But she heard no footsteps in the corridor. She quickly finished the meal. Before her, the steam fading away, lay the elaborate spicy food, the food that she now knew she must not touch.

When her hunger had abated, it seemed that her senses felt clearer. If only she could remember more. "They must think I've eaten the food," she murmured as she crumbled the spiced cake and put most of the meat under the bed.

There were sounds outside the door. Sarke entered. Irene's heart began to pound with fear. I must make him believe I've eaten the food, she thought to herself.

He smiled at her kindly. "And how is the Princess this morning?" he asked.

Irene closed her eyes for a moment, as if she were dizzy. Then she steadied herself on the table. "Sarke?" she asked slowly.

"Yes, I am Sarke, and you are Princess Irene," the tall man said gently. "Now, Irene, do you remember what we talked about last night?"

Irene looked at him blankly.

"It was about your secrets, Princess Irene."

"Secrets?" she asked.

"You will remember, my dear. I think you will stay in your room until you do."

"Very well, Sarke," said Irene dully. She sat on the bed.

"Are you tired, my dear?" asked Sarke.

She nodded.

"We must cut back on the spice. Sometimes the dose is difficult to measure in these barbaric times. Enough to keep you obedient, but there are things that I need for you to remember."

"Yes, Sarke," said Irene, and yawned.

"I will visit you later, my bride."

Irene felt the same surge of fear wash over her, but she knew that she must not show it. Instead she looked wonderingly into Sarke's face and murmured again, "Yes, Sarke."

"Should I stay with her?" asked a guard. "Or ask one of the women to tend to her?"

"Later," snapped Sarke. "I need every available brother and sister for troop formation. We must locate the mutant village before they grow stronger."

The guard saluted. Sarke bent over Irene and touched her cheek lightly with his finger. "One day, my sweet Irene, you will hold out your arms to me, for I will be your lord and husband."

Never that, said a small but strong voice inside Irene's head. She closed her eyes sleepily to avoid Sarke's penetrating gaze. She kept them shut until she heard Sarke and the guard retreat from the room. Then she sat straight up and opened her eyes. Her thoughts were clearer now.

Images of Mommy flickered before her. She had a sudden flash of bright-colored flowers and arching trees. "The secrets," she whispered. "I've got to save them from Sarke!" Sarke had said something about a mutant village. What kind of world had she woken to, she wondered.

"Mommy, where *are* you?" she murmured aloud as she clenched her fists in desperation. She looked around the small ornate room with its single high window and locked door. There was no escape.

The door to Irene's chamber opened. She spun around, thinking it would be the old woman who had so mysteriously appeared, then disappeared. But it was not. The woman who entered was tall and young. She curtsied deeply when her eyes met Irene's. "I have been sent to attend to your needs," she said humbly. "My Princess," she added.

"Please, just call me Irene."

The woman gasped. "No," she stammered. "I could never do that. You are the bride of Sarke, the Princess of the world."

Irene laced her fingers tightly together. She felt acutely discomfited by the woman's tone. "What is your name?" she asked in a friendly manner.

The woman looked blankly at her. "My name?"

"Yes. What do I call you?" explained Irene, trying to sound cheerful and reassuring.

"I had a name once," answered the woman slowly. "I think it was . . . No, Sarke had said that was a dream. He tells us what is real and what is not. I am your sister."

"Sister?"

"Yes. That is what the others call me."

"What others?"

"The other Children. We are the brothers and sisters of the new world."

"And what is Sarke?"

The woman smiled a beatific smile. "Sarke is the Black Regent. He is the one who leads us in the name of the Sleeping Prince. He is the one who tells us what is real and what is not. He is the one chosen to guide us until David awakes."

"David?" gasped Irene as she was assaulted by a stream of memories and images.

· Nineteen ·

One night David was wakened from sleep. "David, there is much to be done," said Willod urgently.

David yawned and peered out of the hut. Everywhere fires had been lit, and men and women were carrying thin woven grass screens and large baskets.

"They're coming! The gathering!" shrilled the old woman, Izza, who had positioned herself on a high rock.

Through the excited babble of voices, David heard

a ruffling, whirring sound. Everywhere people rushed to the fires carrying screens.

Willod rested his hand on David's shoulder. "It is a good night for the gathering," he said with satisfaction. "There is no wind. We will be prepared for the winter."

Above the din David heard the frightened crying of a small child. A little girl had wandered out of her hut and stood bewildered. The whirring became louder.

Suddenly the little girl screamed. The air had become filled with flying beetles, each at least three inches long. Two of the insects became tangled in her hair. She sobbed and pulled at them. David hurried over, soothingly pried the bugs from her head, and carried her back to her hut. "It's all right now," he said gently as he laid her down and covered her with a rabbit-skin blanket. The sides of the hut thrummed with the avalanche of bugs hitting the walls. David waited with the child until she drifted back to sleep, sucking her thumb and twisting a few strands of rabbit fur in her fingers.

Outside the air was thick with brown, furry bodies. Large insects were drawn to the screens that surrounded the fires like panes of glass on a lantern. Frantically they hurled themselves against the screens, lured by the flickering lights. There they wandered stupidly in aimless paths until each screen was blanketed in twisting brown patterns.

As soon as the screen was covered, a team of two or three people would brush the bugs into wicker baskets, splash the baskets with heavily salted water, seal them shut, and suspend them from narrow tripods over the smoke of the flames. A thick smell almost of burning nuts permeated the air. As it only took about five minutes for each screen to become covered, the work was constant.

David stationed himself at a nearby fire and helped brush the bugs into the baskets, and set the screen straight again. The gathering came in waves. There would be brief respites when only a few bugs landed on the screens. Then everyone would laugh and rub their arms or guzzle sweet fermented drink from skin flasks. But the breaks were short, for soon the next wave would start, sending the people running frantically to adjust screens and baskets.

By dawn, seven man-size hampers had been filled with crisp, charred insects. David's arms ached. He shuddered with disgust as he cleared the milk rabbits' enclosure of the . . . "cockroaches"? A word that surfaced from the depths of his mind. But these creatures were bigger, changed, than the pictures he had once seen. By day the insects crawled slowly or lay on their backs, moving their legs in a dazed fashion.

"They only fly at night," explained Willod. "When cold comes, they make a journey to warmer valleys."

"The monarch butterfly, Canadian geese," murmured David half to himself. "And when I wake, it's nothing but this gathering and the reed grass."

"Perhaps you come from a warmer valley," observed Willod thoughtfully.

For a week the gathering flew at night. Then it was over and the skies were clear. Huge panniers were filled with smoked insects. The people began the task of sorting and processing their catch. The fibrous wings were removed, and the bodies of the insects were coarsely chopped and stored in sealed clay baskets for the year's use.

David shivered as a wave of nausea washed over him and he realized, I've been eating bugs. I thought it was nuts, but how could I have thought that? There are no more trees.

In the distance Izza hefted a basket filled to the brim with the dried insects. She scowled at him. Several children scurried after her, picking up what fell, and squealing with delight as they popped the salty brown morsels into their mouths.

What has Mommy done with all the children? a voice inside his head asked. An image of a tall woman with red hair and white skin, dressed in a long jeweled green gown, flashed before his eyes, and a room full of children with large frightened eyes. Beside the woman stood a tall, thin man, dressed in black. *It's dangerous to ask questions*, whispered a girl with long blond hair.

As David fell into the arduous pattern of survival in the village, the dreams began to fade. He hoped one day he would be allowed to become a part of the Demosee and wear the vote. But the vote was inherited, and he had not been born in the village. He now took pride in his friendship with Toom, and learned all he could about the herd and its ways.

The only person in the village who still mistrusted him was Izza. She made it clear that she considered him an enemy. She was a strange old woman. Willod said that when her son was killed by the Children it had given her a sickness of the mind that could not be cured. Even now she wandered for days away from the village in search of him. No one knew where she went, but she always returned. David tried to pity her, but it was hard to feel sorry for someone who clearly hated him.

Then one night the peace ended. It was storytelling time, and the young men of the village were joking that if the girls of David's village were as well formed as he, they would all leave to find it. Suddenly a look-out screamed from the perimeter. "The Children! From the west!"

"Prepare, save what you can," came Willod's voice loud and commanding over the hysterical babble of the people. Men and women grabbed spears. Children hurried into the darkness carrying baskets of food, provisions, and even infants, to hide in the reeds.

There was a loud rumbling that David realized was the hoofbeats of many horses approaching. Lights flickered beyond the perimeter.

"David, help me with the herd," shouted Willod. "They must not kill the herd."

The rabbits were skittish. The does circled their young, and the stags began to snap angrily at each other. A few bashed themselves repeatedly against the woven walls of the enclosure.

A double line of horsemen had entered the village. Some held smoking torches that streamed flame and sparks against the black sky. Their limbs were straight. They were dressed in fine silk and velvet. Some were women with long flowing hair. David stared in disbelief. Why was there something familiar about these people? They weren't demons. They were only—

But his thoughts were interrupted by Willod. "Take the herd beyond the perimeter into the reeds. You will be safe there."

The air was filled with burning and shrieking. David slipped quietly toward the reeds. He whispered encouragement to the animals, who huddled together nervously as they followed his voice.

Suddenly there was a thunderous crashing in the reeds behind him. A tall man in black towered over David. A pendant hung from the jeweled saddle— PUERI OMNIA VICENT.

David could hear the rabbits scrambling in terror

away from the pounding hooves. If only he could stop this man from chasing the blind herd, the village would be saved.

"You thought you could escape me," growled the man. "Nobody escapes me!"

"Sarke!" gasped David.

"You will never be Prince," said the man scornfully. He hurled his spear hard. The sharp point sliced through David's cloak. He felt a sharp pain in his side and arm as the spear pinned him to the ground. He shut his eyes and relaxed every muscle as if dead. It was his only chance.

"And now Irene is all mine! Mine!" David felt the ground shake from the horses hooves, and heard the familiar maniacal laugh that had haunted so many of his dreams.

Irene! The girl with the long golden hair who had haunted his dreams for so many nights.

"No!" he shouted. But the horse and rider had gone.

· *Twenty* ·

There were loud footsteps out in the corridor. Irene scrambled into a sleeping position and feigned a deep sleep. The door burst open.

"Wake her," snapped Sarke's voice impatiently.

Gentle hands shook her and peeled back the silken coverlet. Irene felt a surge of relief that she had returned the flask of water to its hiding place. Slowly she opened her eyes and forced her mouth into a lax smile.

"Sarke," she murmured sleepily.

"Get up."

Why was Sarke so tense? Something was wrong. Something had happened out there to upset him. Had some of the brothers and sisters been killed? No, she answered herself silently. She knew he would not be this nervous about a few deaths. He loved killing. Yes, that was something she remembered. Sarke loved killing. But what was bothering him now?

"Clothe her suitably," he snapped, "and bring her to the Great Hall."

"Yes, Sarke," murmured the cluster of people who had entered her room. Then they all bowed reverently. As if he was some kind of god, thought Irene to herself. Then she realized that the Children, as they called themselves, must also be drugged. They all moved so slowly, and their eyes were glazed and unseeing. I have no friends here, she thought. Nobody is going to help me except for me. And how could she combat the maniacal loyalty they all had for Sarke?

She allowed herself to be dressed, limply moving her limbs at their request. All the while her thoughts were racing. I have to pretend I am still drugged. But I have to listen and watch and learn. If only I could remember the secrets. But it was no use. That memory remained hidden.

When the dressing was complete, they escorted her to the Great Hall, one man walking ahead, one woman on each side of her, and one man walking behind. Like a prisoner, Irene thought, as she tried to mimic their gliding walk.

All too soon they were at the entrance of the Great Hall. The Children parted to form an aisle for her to walk up to the dais. She stared in front of her, imitating the others. Using her peripheral vision, she could see that the Hall was filthy. There was litter and refuse in the corners. A fire had been set in the middle of the room and some sort of meat was cooking. Yet the Children were oblivious to their surroundings. They stood watching Sarke as if participating in a religious ceremony.

Sarke smiled and held out his arms to her as she mounted the dais. Then he gestured for her to stand to one side.

The men and women did not seem to Irene to be quite as beautiful as she had first thought. Their clothing, while jeweled and made of fine cloth, was often torn or dirty. Also, there was an emptiness about their faces that made them almost ugly. On some unseen signal they began speaking in unison. "Wake, David, and come to us. Take your place among us and lead us. Make this barren world a paradise for us to live in. Wake, David. Wake, David."

Somewhere a woman sobbed. Several reeled in their places as if dizzy. Irene darted a glance at Sarke, but he was busy smiling with intensity at his audience. Then he held up his hands, and immediately the confusion stopped.

"Children," he said in a thundering but kindly way, "for years now I have led you, as Regent only, and yet proud of that noble post, waiting with you for the time when our beloved David, our Sleeping Prince, would rise from the prison of this mountain and lead us to the promised paradise." There was a pause, and the crowd moaned.

Sarke raised his hands benevolently and continued. "And I have been honored by my responsibility. When you woke, ten years ago, each one of you woke with the absolute conviction that you must follow the Sleeping Prince. I have tried to care for you until he came to us. I have told you what are dreams and what are not. I have protected you from the evil she-demon who still lurks in this mountain. Last night, as I fought with the mutants, something happened to me."

He paused dramatically. Irene watched the crowd lean forward eagerly. There was a waiting silence.

"My Children, the divine soul of our beloved David entered me, and even now can speak to you through this humble vessel that I call myself." He paused again, and Irene could tell that he was judging the audience to see if they would believe him. Apparently they did, for a wave of hysteria swept over them and they began to scream, "David, David!"

Men and women alike began weeping and embracing each other. Sarke allowed the confusion to continue for some time. Then he spoke again. This time his voice was ominous, and the Children became silent, their eyes frightened.

"But in the mutant hideout there was a boy who called himself David, a boy in league with the she-devil herself!"

"Mommy!" The Children gasped in horror, and someone screamed.

David's alive, thought Irene to herself. David's alive. I've got to find him. I've got to escape from here!

Sarke smiled and his teeth showed white in the firelight. "I fought with him, and I killed him," he said triumphantly.

Irene felt her knees begin to buckle. She staggered a few steps forward. There was a roaring in her ears. Faintly she could hear Sarke's voice in the distance. "Now we must exterminate the mutants once and for all. We cannot allow even a memory of a false David to contaminate this world. I have become David. I am your Prince!" Sarke began to laugh triumphantly.

"David! David!" screamed the Children in a deafening chant.

"David is dead?" whispered Irene in disbelief and shock.

· *Twenty one* ·

David staggered to his feet. He coughed. The air was thick with smoke and burning. His side felt cold and wet. There was red on his fingers. Cautiously he crept forward.

The carefully constructed herd enclosure had been smashed. Beside it lay the twisted figure of Toom. He was covered with blood, and his spear had been shattered. In the end he had fought with his hands, for his fingers and knuckles were bruised and broken. He moaned and opened his eyes.

"David?"

"Yes."

"Take my vote. I give it to you. The herd—" but his voice faltered and ended in a sigh as his muscles gave a final shudder and relaxed.

David kept on holding Toom against him. He was crying. And somehow the pain in his side didn't matter anymore. He felt a hand on his shoulder.

"You are truly part of the village now. Toom has passed on his vote as if you were his son." It was Willod. His face was weary, and there were blood-stains on his cape. He unfastened the pouch that contained the voting stones from Toom's neck, and refastened it about David's neck. "You are now part of the Demosee," he said in a formal tone. "You are part of the present and the future of this village."

David knew that in the pouch lay two stones, one black and one white, and that in the councils that was how the decisions were made—by the people. White for yes, and black for no.

"And you are the herd master now."

David looked around at the smoking wreckage. "Is there a herd left, Willod?"

The man smiled. "Yes. Our children found most of the rabbits wandering in the reeds."

"What about the people?" asked David.

"Luckily few were killed, but many have been wounded. We will flee into the reeds and build a new village. We have done this many times. Most important, the sacred writings of Jahben are safe. As long as we have them, the Demosee will endure."

By dawn what had once been the village was empty. The people spoke softly and crept low to the ground as they collected their belongings and made ready for the journey. Many of the baskets containing the precious gathering had been destroyed. The people faced a hungry and cold winter.

They traveled by night and slept by day. Rations were meager. Each person received a handful of *trageth*, a mixture of the salty brown gathering and grain.

The children chewed reed stems as they walked, to quell their hunger.

David insisted that the female breed rabbits be fed portions of grain daily to keep up their strength. There was some grumbling at this, but everyone knew the importance of the herd.

For the most part, the journey was made in silence. Even the babies had stopped crying and only occasionally whimpered in their mothers' arms. Just before dawn Willod would hold up his hand in the air, and the company would collapse in exhaustion on the cold ground.

David slept little. The rabbits were unaccustomed to the night schedule, and spent much of the day nibbling at the reeds. He was forced to watch them closely to make sure they did not wander off, and also to check for signs of stress. Already the milk rabbits were drying up, and several of the stags were losing fur in bunches along their backs and sides.

The people were terrified that the Sleeping Prince had awoken and would pursue them through the reeds. One woman who had been hiding in the reeds had heard the Black Regent muttering as he bent down to slash at a hut that the time had come for the Prince to claim his power.

Some whispered that the Prince feasted on human blood, and if a dark cloud was blown quickly over the moon, the people would look up and cross their hands over their heads in a gesture that symbolized protection from evil forces.

Willod seemed tireless. He woke each person gently at night, and when he handed out the portions of *trageth*, he spoke words of hope and encouragement. Those who had been wounded received special attention. He was also concerned about the herd being stressed by the journey. One day, as the people slept, he fashioned a small litter with high sides and lined it with grass for the milk-producing rabbits to ride in.

Scouts were sent out in all directions. The report came that although the Children had returned to the mountain, the digging had stopped. "The Prince has indeed awoken," said Izza with grim satisfaction.

"Did you see the Prince?" queried Willod. The scout shook his head.

"He is made of air," crooned Izza. "And in the night he turns to flesh and blood to suck the life out of living things. The herd is weakening. He is draining the life from our rabbits. Toom would not have let this happen."

"The herd always weakens when we journey," answered Willod sharply.

"He's one of them," mouthed Izza, her yellow teeth glinting through her cracked lips as she stared at David. "He led them to find us."

David tried to ignore the old woman, but as the journey continued, more and more of the people were seen clustered about her, listening with intense fascination to her dark stories.

"The Prince has awoken at last. The evil is complete. Darkness will cover the world. Dahben will never come to us now. We would be wise to kill our own children before they can be enslaved by the wickedness that will consume everything, leaving a trail of blood that can never dry."

David watched several of the children slink away from the circle in terror. Willod shook his head sadly. "Don't worry," he said. "The people would never kill their own children because of the words of one old woman."

"How much farther must we travel?" asked David.

"Two more days. It is not easy finding a site for the village. There must be clean water, untainted grazing for the herd, a land formation that hides us from our enemies, and a place that is visited by the gathering. Also, Jahben has forbidden us to settle further than a week's walk from the mountain. He said that Dahben must be able to find us when he wakes. I hope these rumors about the Sleeping Prince are false. The village cannot survive another attack," he added grimly.

David was glad when after two days Willod announced that the land was safe, and the journey over. But before any huts could be built, a herd enclosure must be fashioned. David supervised the proceedings

carefully. He was concerned that several of the rabbits had sickened, and he insisted that the walls be
made high and thick to keep out the chilling wind.

Spirits were higher. Izza seemed angry that fewer
of the people gathered about to hear her, but everyone was busy erecting shelters and exploring the new
site.

That night there was a meeting of the Demosee
for David to be officially welcomed as a new member
of the village. It was an important ceremony. David
stood tall before the smoking fire. The night air was
cold, but he had stripped to the waist to show that
he wore the vote about his neck.

"We welcome David to the Demosee," said Willod
in a loud voice. "He came as a stranger, from another
village. Although we have had to flee again from the
Children, and although we look forward to a long
winter, this is a time for celebration. David is proof
that there is another village somewhere, and we are
not alone. David and Toom saved the herd from the
Children, and it is with pride and gratitude that I
welcome David to the Demosee."

Izza pushed her way into the circle. She laughed
derisively as she surveyed the assembly. "That's right
Willod, welcome a spy from the Black Regent!" She
spat noisily.

"Izza!" thundered Willod.

"I have the right of free speech. Your precious Jahben says that everyone must have the right to speak

in the Demosee. Well, let me tell you," her voice
became a snarling sing-song. "He came dressed like
one of them. He says he doesn't remember. But he
has the look of them. His face and limbs are from the
Time-Before. And you would give him the task of
herd master. You fool. The Children of Time drink
blood. He'll drain the herd one by one, and then he'll
start sucking our blood."

The crowd rustled uneasily. "You have no proof of
this," someone shouted. "Maybe she's right," muttered another.

"I want a vote," screeched Izza.

Willod tossed a cape to David. "We will vote tomorrow night. For Jahben has said there will be no
vote taken without the proper time to think." He
shook his head angrily. "Izza, you have falsely ac-
cused one of our people. I believe that David is completely within his rights to charge you with speaking
lies against him. Tomorrow night the Demosee will
be voting on that also."

"We shall see," snarled Izza. "We shall see."

Whispering among themselves, the people withdrew to their huts. David and Willod stood before the
dying fire.

"Watch the herd well tonight," said Willod in a
low voice.

"Surely no one would hurt the rabbits," answered
David. "The village depends on them for so much."

"Watch them closely all the same," said Willod.

"Perhaps this journey has upset Izza more than I guessed. She is very old."

David smiled. "Don't worry, Willod. I will not accuse her of lies against me. She may hate me, but she is part of the village. There has been enough death here."

Willod nodded. "That sounds like something Jahben may have said. To me you are already a member of the Demosee."

Willod clasped David's hand firmly, and the two looked straight into each other's eyes. Then David turned and went back to the herd enclosure.

In spite of his words to Willod, David was indeed worried that Izza might harm the rabbits. So he resolved to stay awake through the night to protect them. He crept into the shelter and called them in.

They hopped slowly into the lean-to. David pulled his blankets around him, and soon several of the huge brown furry creatures lay resting beside him. He stroked the head stag's neck gently and wondered what these blind animals thought about, or if they, like him, dreamed when they slept. One of the milk rabbits hopped lazily into his lap and pushed her nose under his hand demandingly. David stroked her gently. A short distance away he could hear another rabbit chewing methodically on some reeds.

Several hours passed. The furry bodies were warm against him. David was very tired. It was hard to stay awake.

Suddenly he heard a noise outside the shelter. It sounded like someone or something trying to get in. He stumbled to his feet. Disturbed, the rabbits hopped in slow circles, moving their sightless heads back and forth in distress.

"Shhh, it's okay, it's okay," whispered David reassuringly. He stepped out into the cold dark. The reeds crackled under his feet. "Who's there?" he called. There was no answer. A stick snapped. "Who's there?" he called again as he walked toward the sound.

Suddenly something hit his head from behind. There was a flash of light inside his brain as he sank to his knees. He was hit again. This time he fell forward, unconscious.

In the shelter the blind rabbits hopped nervously about, sniffing the night air for intruders.

·*Twenty two*·

Irene was led back to her room—her prison cell, she thought bitterly—by several of the women. The religious fervor had left them, and they moved slowly, each with a lazy, dreaming expression on her face. She feigned exhaustion, and they left her, locking the door behind them.

As soon as she was alone, Irene scrambled up and began pacing about the room. She knew the time of her wedding with Sarke was fast approaching—especially now that he had "become David," as he put it. The shock of learning that David had been alive but now was lying brutally murdered had jolted her memory into returning.

As she nervously walked to and fro, a flood of images bombarded her. It was almost as if she were seeing her own life for the first time, as a bystander. Faces that had been forgotten became crystal clear. She saw her own mother and father clearly, the wrinkles on her father's face, the nervous way her mother kept brushing back her hair with her thin hands. "And I wasn't six, I was ten," she muttered. Why had she been so eager to believe Mommy. She could hear Mommy's persuasive voice. "Irene, you have been very sick. It is hard for a small child to lose both parents in such a terrible accident."

Irene remembered now, staring up at Mommy and saying, "I'm not a small child. I'm ten years old."

"You're mind is not strong, dear. I will take care of you. Please call me Mommy. I am your mother now, and you are six years old. When you are ten years old, I will tell you."

Then came the dizziness and the frightening dreams, but when she called the strange woman, "Mommy," the dreams disappeared, and the walls became steady. She remembered how David had fought Mommy, even to the end, trying to escape, trying to make her remember her real parents. She had hated him for doing that. Now she knew he was right. But it was too late to tell him so.

How many years had she lived in the castle, fearing and loving the Lady Anastasia? She heard herself saying to David, "She loves you, that's why she punishes you!" Worse, she remembered really believing it, not understanding David's anger and indignation. She had felt so hurt and concerned that he didn't love Mommy and was questioning Mommy's right to punish and destroy children.

Irene spoke aloud as if David stood before her. "I'm sorry, David. I was here for so many years. I had stopped thinking for myself. I really. . . believed Mommy."

And yet that was why Mommy had picked her in the first place—thinking. The ability to solve problems. That was how Mommy picked all of her children, physical and mental achievement. Irene had won a gold in the Intellectual Olympics, Twelve and Under Decathlon division—the President himself had called her. She had been awarded a scholarship to study agricultural research in a special think tank for exceptional children. Then, a year later, there was no president, the farm had been sold, they had moved to the Northern Sector, and the mine collapsed, killing both her parents.

Agriculture! Finally she remembered what her pre-

cious *secrets* were and why Sarke wanted them so badly,
why they were so important. Seeds. Seeds of fruit-
giving trees, grains, shrubs, and flowers. Seeds that
had taken years of research to prepare for extended
dormancy and to make radiation-resistant. Not even
Mommy knew or understood the delicate procedures
that each one required to become viable. The destroyed Earth *could* become a lush green garden. But
only through me, thought Irene. The question was,
where had Mommy hidden them? Somehow she had
to get them back.

There was a rush of cold air at Irene's back. She
turned quickly. The old hag stood there, reaching out
with her clawlike hands. "My precious child," whispered the figure. "I have come back to take care of
you. I will always take care of you."

"Mommy?" asked Irene hesitantly.

·*Twenty three*·

"Irene, my precious little girl. My darling child,"
cackled the crone happily and she rushed to embrace
Irene. Irene took a step back. She was remembering
the punishments that she had endured, the terrible

dreams, the cruelty. She also remembered the kill-
ings.

"I am old now. But you will love me just the same.
You always were loyal to me. I tested you, and you
remained loyal. I test all my children. But you were
my first. A mother always has special feelings toward
her first-born."

Irene wanted to say, "You are not my mother," but
she knew better than to anger Mommy. Mommy was
the only one who knew where the secrets were. So
instead she said, "Sarke has killed David."

Mommy shook her head sadly. "I tried to save him,
Irene. I knew you had special feelings toward him."

Irene flushed and turned away. Whatever feelings
she may have had toward David were irrelevant. He
was dead. But he would have wanted her to share the
secrets with the world if he had known what they
were.

Mommy was staring at her intensely. All that remained of her striking beauty were her lavender eyes,
which glistened behind the wrinkles and filth that
covered her face. "David was part of my plan for you.
The Prince marries the Princess, so sweet, so innocent, and I would be watching and guiding.

"But Sarke was close to finding David's chamber.
I had to break my poor little Prince, my little boy
blue out of hybe much too quickly. His brain was
damaged. He's useless to me now. Nevertheless, he

was one of my children, so I did the best I could for him. I set him free on the mountain. If Sarke found him, so be it. Besides, he never loved me the way you do, my precious Irene. You do love me, don't you?"

Irene tried to make her voice as gentle as possible. "Yes, Mommy, I love you very much. Now, where did you hide my secrets?"

·Twenty four·

David opened his eyes. It was dawn. His body was numb with cold and his head ached. He staggered to his feet. "The herd," he mumbled. "I have to check the herd." One of the rabbits hopped slowly up to him. David could see several of the animals munching on the reeds. He tried to count, but his vision blurred. I must find Willod, he thought.

Still rubbing his head, he slipped out through the enclosure, then paused in his tracks. Izza was approaching, and behind her, several of the villagers. Their features were contorted with anger, and they carried the limp bodies of two rabbits.

"See, he drinks their blood," screamed Izza sharply. "There's blood on his mouth!"

David touched the back of his hand to his face. It was wet and sticky. Then he looked at the rabbits. "You killed them?" he whispered in disbelief. "You hate me that much?" He reached out to take the dead animals.

"Don't let him touch them. He'll poison the herd," shrieked the old woman.

Willod strode quickly throughout the crowd. "What's going on here?" he asked. Wordlessly, one of the men held up a carcass.

"I told you so," hissed Izza. "You wouldn't listen to me. My son should have been herd master, my Larth."

"Larth has been dead for three years. Don't you remember?"

"He lives! My Larth is the rightful herd master!" screamed Izza.

Willod turned from her to David. "What happened here? Why is there blood on your face? Are you hurt?"

"I—" began David.

But Izza interrupted him. "He's been drinking the blood of the herd. That's why they weakened. Soon he'll be drinking our blood, and we'll die one by one. He killed my Larth so that he could be herd master."

"That's not true," said David hotly. "I would never hurt the rabbits. Someone hit me on the head." He tried to take the dead animals from the people, but they drew back from him in terror.

"This is a matter for the Demosee," said Willod in a loud voice.

"No!" retorted Izza. "The Demosee has failed. The boy's a spy. That's why they found our village. We should kill him now before he kills us the way he killed my own precious Larth."

"The writings of Jahben," began Willod sternly.

"Your Jahben was a fool. He never said anything about the Sleeping Prince. It's all lies. But we know the Children are real and their Prince is real too."

"This is a matter to be voted on," said Willod in a loud voice.

"But the blood on his face," murmured someone in the crowd.

"They are both in league with the Children! Kill them both quickly!" screamed Izza.

Willod held up his arms for silence, but the crowd was out of control and had begun surging toward them. He glanced quickly at David, and then in a thundering voice he said, "Begone, David, bringer of evil to the Demosee. And never return to this village!"

There was loud screaming in the crowd. Willod made a wild gesture in the air and placed his hand on David's shoulder. "Go quickly," he said in an undertone. "I know you are not guilty. But I fear for your life. This is the only way."

David saw understanding and pain in Willod's face.

He nodded, then turned and ran toward the perimeter.

"Kill him," screamed Izza. "Kill him!"

"No," bellowed Willod above the chaos. "That will only release his evil spirit. As leader, I have banished him from our village so that the way of the Demosee might return."

There was a silence. Then he dropped his hands to his sides. "Or kill me if you wish. I realize now that I have failed Jahben. However, whether I remain your leader or not, I will continue to believe that someday Dahben will come to us, even if I am the only one who believes in him."

"No, you are our leader, Willod. The way of the Demosee is right. And you have saved us from evil," said someone in the crowd. There was a muttering of agreement.

But Willod shook his head sadly and walked alone to the perimeter, where he spent a long time staring out toward the faraway mountain.

The frozen muck of the swamps bruised David's feet as he ran through the reeds. He knew Willod had risked much to save him, and he hoped the leader was safe. However, as he ran, his head began to clear, and he realized that the blow to his head had jarred into place many memories of past lives. He had to get back to the mountain. Something had gone terribly wrong with Mommy's plans, and Sarke was at the bottom of it.

How had the others awoken ten years before him?
Where was Irene? Was she a woman now? He began
to remember how Sarke's eyes followed Irene when
she walked. If she lived, she was in great danger.
Where was Mommy? Had Sarke killed her?

David traveled quickly toward the mountain. He
left no traces for the village scouts to find. The trek
with the villagers had been an arduous journey. The
herd tired easily, and the people were sick and frightened.

Alone, David made good speed. His legs moved of
their own accord. He was banished from the village,
and the world he had dreamed of so many times no
longer existed. It was almost as if the ground were
being ripped from under his feet with each step as
he stood still remembering and remembering. Tears
kept welling up behind his eyes in a dull ache. Even
if his parents had somehow survived the end, they
were long dead now.

He glanced up at the dark sky. Already, a few stars
lay patterned against the vast blackness. The memory of Irene surfaced again. He could almost feel the
gentle touch of her hand on his arm, and hear her
voice. He knew he had to find her. She would never
follow Sarke . . . willingly.

But as he walked toward the dark shadow of the
mountain, he found himself wondering how ten years
would have changed her. Could anyone hold out a-
gainst Sarke for ten years?

Soon the mountain loomed over him, ugly and threatening. A horse whinnied and stamped close by. David froze in his tracks. But the horse was riderless, tethered on a long cord to feed in the reed grass.

A lone sentry guarded one of the lower entrances. The man seemed in some sort of trance, and it was easy for David to slip past unnoticed. Inside, the well-ordered halls of the castle were lined with sleeping men and women. There was filth everywhere and an unclean smell that seemed to thicken the air. David made his way to the Great Hall. If any of the Children noticed him, they simply turned their head and sank back into sleep. He remembered a hiding place between two carved stone pillars and wedged himself between them, knowing that in the flickering torchlight, he was all but invisible to the rest of the room.

He dozed standing. A slave set a fire and began turning a large chunk of meat on a spit. David wondered if it was horse or rabbit. He couldn't help hoping it was the former.

Sarke strode into the hall. In contrast to his followers, his black cape and tunic were sparkling and clean. His face was smooth and almost polished. By now the slave had cut the meat into pieces and was stirring it into a huge iron pot. Sarke cuffed him, so that he sprawled against the floor, then poked into the pot with a ladle. He ate quickly and noisily. When he had finished, he kicked the slave again "for watching him." The slave turned away, and Sarke, after glanc-

ing about in a curiously furtive way, dumped into the
pot the contents of a small pouch that he drew out
from under his cape. Then he smiled a satisfied smile
and left the hall. The slave scrambled to his feet and
resumed stirring the pot.

Suddenly Sarke reappeared. He made a sign with
his hand, and a slave began to bang on a huge gong
that hung suspended over one of the archways. Presently the Children began to assemble. They arranged
themselves in rows before the dais on which Sarke
stood. David tried to match the faces of the men and
women with the boys and girls he had known so well,
but the hall was dim, and too much time had passed.

Sarke smiled at them kindly and motioned for them
to eat their fill from the black caldron. Obediently
they trooped to the fire, and each held out a bowl to
be filled. They ate of the stew greedily. Some even
brought the empty bowls up to their faces and licked
up the last traces of gravy with their tongues. But
they spoke not a word, nor even exchanged a glance
with one another. When they had finished, they arranged themselves again in the rows before the dais,
each person in the same place as before.

Sarke began to speak. His voice was clear and
compelling. He began by telling the Children how
perfect they were and how proud he was of them.
"But now for the battle plans—" he said. He raised
his hand, and a figure emerged from the other side

of the dais. It was a woman, old and bent over. David could not see her face.

"Beloved daughter of shadows," said Sarke warmly. "Many times you have revealed your village to me."

A shiny drop of saliva worked its way out of the corner of the old woman's mouth. She pressed her fingers against her chest. "Please, my lord," she intoned. "Please let me see my son, my Larth, whom you have made whole and clean."

Sarke smiled kindly at her. "Yes, Izza. Larth is pure now. He waits for you patiently. But you are still a mutant."

Izza turned her face toward the rows of silent Children, her eyes searching for her son. Sarke turned her face back to him. "You must tell us where the village is, and of the impostor."

"I never believed him to be the true Prince," jabbered Izza. "He called himself by the sacred name, David, that only you know. But I knew him to be false."

"Where has the village moved, Izza?" David shuddered at the cruelty of the man's voice.

A slave brought a map. "You remember about maps, don't you, Izza. I have taught you how to read them. And you will show us where to find the mutants."

Anxiously, Izza studied the map, running her fingers over its surface. David could feel Sarke's impatience growing. Finally, her finger was still. "It is here," she whispered. She looked beseechingly up at Sarke. "And my son?"

Sarke took her hands in his. "You are a mutant, Izza. Your pure and perfect soul of shadows is trapped forever in a mutant's body."

"Larth is ashamed of me?" Izza's voice became querulous.

In spite of himself, David felt a surge of pity for the old woman. She was nothing but a helpless pawn in Sarke's hands.

"How can I help you, Izza?" asked Sarke quietly. "Only you know what needs to be done."

A sickening realization washed over David. "No!" he wanted to shout. He began to slide from his hiding place. But at that moment Izza walked toward the edge of the dais with her hands outstretched. "Release me!" screamed the old woman. "Give me a new body so that I can see my Larth."

The crowd began to stir. "It is the first blood of the kill!" thundered Sarke. "The willing sacrifice."

"Release me!" screamed the woman again.

David did not watch as the Children climbed the stage and the killing began.

When the noise and shouts ended, he knew it was over. He kept his face turned away. He also knew that Sarke was smiling, his white teeth glinting in the torchlight.

Sarke began speaking again. "Now, my Children. The spirit of our divine David has entered me, and it is he who now speaks. Tomorrow we will ride out to the village and destroy the vermin forever. But first, I will celebrate my wedding rites with the Princess Irene."

·*Twenty five*·

Mommy smiled at Irene, her lavender eyes glinting. "Sarke will never find your secrets. I will take you there, my precious child. I—"

There was a sound at the door. A young woman entered carrying a tray of food. Although she was different from the woman before, her eyes held the same vacant stare. When Irene turned back to Mommy, the old woman had vanished.

"My Princess," said the woman humbly.

Irene turned toward her slowly. "Yes, sister?" she said in a slow voice. She noticed with distaste that the woman's gown was spattered with reddish-brown stains.

"I have come to dress you for your sacred wedding to our Sarke, our Sarke who has become David, Sarke who is one with the Prince who will turn this world into a paradise."

"Now?" Irene's heart had begun pounding. She tried to breathe, but her lungs refused to expand.

"It is a blessed day," said the woman euphorically.

"I . . . I don't know if I'm strong enough," said Irene as she lay back on the bed and shut her eyes. *How can I stall for time? I've got to stall for time. I can't marry Sarke. I'm not old enough to marry anybody.* Her thoughts were loud and shrill in her head. Suddenly she began laughing uncontrollably. *What am I thinking? I'm hundreds of years old. I don't even know how old I was before the destruction!*

"Princess?" asked the woman in a perplexed voice.

"I was laughing," answered Irene, trying to relax her face into a mindless emptiness.

"Laughing?" The woman seemed puzzled. Then she nodded hesitantly. "Yes . . . Sarke, now David, sometimes laughs. Are you tired, Princess Irene? I have brought you food and drink. He-that-was-Sarke has commanded that you be fed before your wedding."

"I'm not hungry . . . sister," Irene added.

"Then we will prepare you for the marriage rites."

The small chamber became filled with the beautiful young women. Reverently they peeled off her silken tunic. She closed her eyes and lay back on the bed, naked. She knew there was nothing to fear from them. They treated her as an object of worship. The room was silent as they bathed her, then rubbed her with sweet smelling ointment. Irene forced herself to relax. She didn't want them touching her. Yet their touch was impersonal and gentle.

A beautiful white silk gown was brought. It twinkled and shimmered with pearls and tiny diamonds. Soon she stood before them, dressed in white.

A man brought a jeweled goblet, and bowing, held it out to her. Irene could smell the spicy tang of the wine. She smiled and shook her head.

"Sarke says you are to drink this before the wedding." Irene noticed that his cape was also spattered with the reddish-brown stain of fresh blood. Her eyes moved back to the goblet.

"But surely if I drink this, I will sleep . . . my brother," she added. She recognized panic forming in the man's expressionless eyes. He was terrified of failing his master.

"Sarke commanded me to give this to you," he insisted harshly. He now was pushing the goblet at her lips.

"No," she began to say, and tried to push the goblet away.

"But Sarke ordered me! Sarke ordered me!" he repeated in a frenzied voice. Roughly he grabbed Irene by the back of her neck and forced the goblet to her lips. "Sarke ordered me, Sarke ordered me," she heard the man yelling.

Irene gagged as she swallowed the spiced wine. Finally, she managed to push the man away, and threw the goblet to the floor. Red wine had spilled down the front of her white dress. The other men and women simply stared calmly at her, and now suddenly, the man who had made her drink was calm again also. It was as if he had forgotten his anger.

Presently she became very dizzy. At least I drank only half, she thought to herself. But the words inside her head seemed like strange isolated bubbles without meaning.

"Come Princess Irene, it is time for your wedding," said one of them.

"Blessed Princess, accept your happiness. Soon you will be joined with He-that-was-Sarke, our David. The world will become our paradise, and all that Sarke has foretold will come true. Blessed Princess, how fortunate you are to have been chosen. And he will cherish you forever."

Irene found it was easy to smile. The walls of her chamber swam and rippled. Gentle hands caught her, and then she was walking down a stone corridor, into the Great Hall, and at the end of it all, Sarke was waiting.

·*Twenty six*·

David, still crouched between the pillars, saw Irene escorted down the center of the huge Great Hall. She staggered and was supported by the group who attended her. As she passed, quite close to his hiding place, he saw with relief that she was still young. She was the same Irene. She had not aged into a grown woman. But her eyes—her eyes were empty and without expression How could Sarke do this to her? he raged silently.

Sarke had appeared on the dais and held out his arms to welcome Irene. She walked slowly to him, then stood to one side.

"My beloved Children," spoke Sarke. "This is the first marriage, the promised marriage that will turn this wasteland into a paradise." He turned toward Irene. "As David, for his spirit is within me, I beseech you, Princess Irene, to become my fair wife and consort."

Irene stared at him, her eyes blank. "Yes, of course. Whatever you wish," she said.

"Then the Prince has become a king, and the Princess a queen. Come, my pretty Irene, to the bridal chamber. It has been specially prepared for you. I have waited a long time for this."

The Children began chanting some sort of ritualistic rhyme about the promise of paradise. Sarke took Irene's hand.

This simple gesture jarred David from his shock, and he burst from his hiding place. "No, Irene!" he shouted as he leapt toward the dais.

Irene started. "David!" she screamed as she looked around wildly. For a brief moment her eyes cleared and the room snapped into focus.

Sarke towered over her. "You are mine," he whispered hoarsely. "Tell them you are mine forever! This is the evil impostor. Reject him." He began stroking Irene's cheek with his huge white hand.

Irene stared at David. She was pale, and her eyes still unfocused. Then, reaching for Sarke's hand, she pulled it close to her mouth. He grinned in satisfaction and triumph, but only for a moment—because Irene sank her teeth hard and fast into his flesh. He gave an angry cry and yanked back his hand. "Never, Sarke!" she hissed. "I will *never* be yours."

The room was silent.

"Then you will die, sweet Irene. And I will watch you die." Then he raised his hands above his head. "My Children," he shouted. "My beloved Children. The impostor must be killed. He has tainted my bride and they must both be punished. Let the rite of sacrifice and purification begin." He jumped down onto the main floor and pointed at Irene and David.

The Children began moving toward the dais. David remembered the killing of Izza. Irene remembered the blood stains on the Children's garments. They stood shoulder to shoulder as the Children closed in on them.

"Irene, I'm sorry," whispered David.

"David I—"

But at that moment there was a loud scornful laugh. "Now listen, my sweet Children, for you are mine and always have been."

There was silence. Then some of the Children began screaming and covering their eyes. Sarke looked angrily about, but the speaker was invisible, and her familiar voice seemed to issue from every pillar and arch.

"You would kill your own Prince and Princess at the whim of Sarke? You don't love me, any of you, and now you will have to pay. I will take them away from you forever, and you will *never* have the kingdom I promised you. *Never!* I will watch you sicken and rot in your own nightmares. Perhaps the mutants will prove more deserving of my kindness."

Suddenly Mommy appeared on the dais and grabbed Irene and David in her strong, clawlike grip. "Hurry!" she muttered as she yanked them backward. For a moment David felt the familiar tingle of a holo-door, then they were surrounded by darkness. He could hear Sarke's voice above the din of screams and sobbing.

"We will find the village. We will kill them all. We will wipe them out down to the last mewling offspring. Then the world will be pure again. I killed the impostor once in the mutant village. Even now he is fleeing there with the Princess and the she-devil, hoping to find protection among the mutants. But all they will find is a heap of burning ashes! Prepare to ride!"

David hesitated. The village could not withstand another attack. He had to warn Willod somehow. But at the same time, he couldn't leave Irene to the mercy of Mommy. He hastened after her hunched-over form, trying to hold Irene so that she would not stumble on the winding way.

"He tried to trick me. I woke all alone. He thought I would be dead. But I know more than he does. I've kept myself alive. You have done well, my sweet Prince. I thought you might never think again. I had to rip you out of your hybe unit too quickly. I had to get you away from Sarke. Say, thank you, Mommy."

"Where are we going, Mommy?" asked David, trying to keep the loathing from his voice. He remembered her, her lavender eyes, her white skin, and her cruelty. A dull light gleamed in the passage as they followed the old woman.

"Safe, my little boy blue, safe. Mommy always

protects her children. It's just the three of us now. I
have the Prince and the Princess all to myself. I know
all the hidden places. They'll never find us." She
motioned with her hand, and the solid wall of stone
dissolved into a door.

They were in a dark room with crumbling walls.
An iron faucet dripped water into a pail. There was a
smell of wet stone and mold. "I have pure water here.
You don't find much of that in the castle—except for
the horses and slaves. Oh, my darling David." She
reached out her arms toward him.

He stepped back to avoid her touch. "Are you okay,
Irene?" he asked.

Mommy laughed scornfully. "She has been given
a heavy dose of Sarke's drugs. She'll believe anything
anyone tells her, and it will become part of her thinking even after the drugs have worn off. She's a recep-
tive child. She always has been."

David put his hand gently on Irene's arm. "Let's
get out of here, Irene."

Irene looked slowly from David to Mommy. "I
can't," she said finally in a low voice.

"What do you mean, you can't?"

She shook her head.

David flung up his hands in exasperation. "Irene,
outside there's a whole other life. Please come with
me."

"So you're leaving me, David?" Mommy's voice
was bitter. "You never loved me. You're just like the

rest of them. Go away, both of you. I'll have my re-
venge. I always win. You know I always win."

Irene walked slowly over and stood beside the old
woman. "I won't leave you, Mommy," she said softly.
"I love you."

David felt a surge of anger so intense that his eyes
pricked with unshed tears and his chest hurt. He had
dreamed of Irene with her golden hair and her gentle
voice so often that it was almost as if she were a part
of him. But she was choosing Mommy. After all the
cruelty and the lies. He tried to feel pity for her. It
wasn't her fault that she had been at the mercy of
Mommy for so long, but somehow he wished she had
taken a stand, the way she did with Sarke. He shook
his head sadly. "Good-bye then. I would have done
anything for you. But you never change. You will go
on obeying Mommy until you die."

Irene remained silent. David turned on his heel
and left the dimly lighted chamber. He could feel her
staring after him, her eyes entreating him to understand. He knew her face wore that expression of hurt
fear. But it was too late. He would not stay, and he
would not play Mommy's games ever again. Behind
him the door faded and the wall became solid.

He retraced his steps and found his way to the in-
habited part of the castle, where he picked up an
embroidered cloak and pulled the hood down over
his eyes. In the debris that lined the halls he found

a sword and jeweled belt. As he strapped it to his waist, one of the Children staggered into him. His eyes met David's. For a moment David feared that he would be revealed, but the man only said, "Do I know you, brother? But forgive me, sometimes I remember dreams. I am unworthy of Sarke's compassion."

David shook his head slowly. He knew he had to concentrate on merging with the army. He could never reach the village on foot before Sarke, and a horse would be too easily missed. He forced his feelings of rage at Irene and Mommy aside. The only thing left was to preserve the village at all costs.

The Children were calm now, as if they had already forgotten their fear. Slaves brought horses, all freshly groomed and saddled. David scanned the mounts and chose a white mare that seemed quick and gentle. A slave child held the bridle while he mounted. One of the Children approached. "That is my horse," he said in a puzzled voice.

David looked gently down at him. "No, brother," he answered, using the same quiet tone that he had heard so often. "You are remembering a dream. Be at peace, and one with Sarke."

The man nodded. "Forgive me, brother," he said apologetically. "You are right. It is the dreams. I cannot tell them apart somehow." The man wandered off in search of another horse.

The slave child gave David a piercing look, but
David simply smiled and nodded at him as he gathered up the reins and rode to where the rest of Sarke's
army was waiting.

·*Twenty seven*·

The old woman leaned against the wall and covered
her face with her hands, her breathing punctuated by
rasping sobs. "How could he hate me so much? I was
a good mother to him. I have failed. And I am so
old. All those years of waiting while the Children slept.
Alone. Feeling my body age, become weak and sicken.
I kept myself alive for you, my darling daughter, my
first-born. You were the first—so young, so innocent."
The hunched-over body shook with a loud spasm of
coughing. She pushed the back of her hand against
her mouth, and when she dropped it, it glistened with
red. "I haven't much time left, my sweet Princess.
We must pay them back for what they've done to
me." Her breath was uneven now. "I have sealed us
in. We will die together, my sweet Irene."

"What about my secrets?" asked Irene quietly.

"They're here!" gloated Mommy. "I've kept them
hidden all these years. Come." She pulled Irene across

the room and pulled out a small trunk from an alcove. "They'll never have them now, will they, Irene?"

Irene shook her head. "No, Mommy."

Mommy smiled, then the coughing shook her again. She gasped and struggled for breath. "I think I am dying now. I know about death. I have watched people die. But I haven't made them pay enough. I wanted to haunt their dreams and make them suffer and scream for betraying me. And I wanted to kill Sarke myself. Take your secrets my child. You may watch me die. Think of it as a lesson. You will die soon yourself. Only I know the door from this room. They'll never have you, and they'll never have paradise."

Irene slowly picked up the metal chest and stood before Mommy. She could feel the effect of the drugs. It made it hard to think clearly or even to think at all. But she had always obeyed Mommy in the past. "You're my mother. I will do whatever you want me to do," she said slowly. It was difficult to form words. Her tongue was fuzzy and thick.

"I want them to suffer," whispered the old woman as she began to crumple down. "They haven't paid enough for their sins."

"No, Mommy. When you die, they will forget you. I am the only one who remembers."

Mommy twitched her head sharply and stared at Irene. "Forget me?" she hissed. "I want them to fear me always. Irene," Mommy spoke quickly and eagerly now, "they must not forget me. Here—" She scrambled toward the wall and made a single scrabbling motion with her fingers. Instantly the door appeared and gaped open. "Irene," she gasped, and her fingers caught the white pearled gown. "You must make them remember me. You must make them pay. You must become the 'Mommy' that they fear. Yes, that's it. You become me! The divine mother. They are our children, but they must be punished!"

Irene gripped the heavy trunk and stared down at the dying woman whom she had known and loved for so many years. Her eyes were still blurring and her body was numb from the drug. She smiled slowly and said the words that were expected of her. . . . "Yes, Mommy, of course."

But the old woman did not hear her, for the lavender eyes had become glazed over with death.

Sarke moved his army out in strict formation. The Children rode well, and the horses were used to moving in tight patterns. As the sun rose, the light bounced and glinted off the jewels and steel sword blades. All around David were the sounds of hooves thudding on frozen ground, the snap of breaking reeds, the jingle of metal, the squeak of leather harness, and the soft grunts of galloping horses.

Sarke rode at the head. Slightly behind him two of the Children carried long, flapping banners with the familiar words *Pueri omnia vicent.*

David found his mind flooded with memories that danced before his eyes with a speed much greater then the passing landscape. He remembered his father and mother clearly, and the world that had been destroyed so long ago. He remembered cities and pavements and the mechanized support systems that nurtured humanity like a metal womb. Trees and flowers and wildlife had flourished where now there were only reed swamps filled with hidden quicksand pockets.

Sarke raised his hand, and the Children reined in their horses to a standstill. There was fumbling in the saddlebags as many pulled out clubs wrapped with oil-soaked cloth and lit them. Damn Izza! For all her insane rantings, she had marked the flight with scientific precision. David knew he had to reach the village first, but how could he break out of the formation?

Sarke was speaking. "Take no prisoners. This time I want the village annihilated. Save the rabbits if you can. I have been too merciful in the past, allowing enough of the mutants to live and move elsewhere, or taking them as slaves. There will be no more of that. When we have finished here, nothing lives!" He bellowed as he dropped his hand, and the army charged forward.

In seconds they were upon the village. A torch was tossed in the herd enclosure. David saw the huge blind rabbits kicking out in fear as the straw ignited and began to hiss and smoke. All around was the sound of screaming.

If only I could get close enough to Sarke, I could kill him from behind, he thought. He kicked his horse hard. But as the horse snorted and reared up, a small boy stumbled in front of him. The boy looked up with fear in his eyes, as if he expected death. But when he saw David, his expression turned to bewilderment. Another of the Children drew her sword and lunged at the child eagerly. Without thinking, David leaned down and swept the boy up behind him. "Hold on," he whispered.

"You're David," murmured the boy, and his grip tightened about David's waist. David held his sword above his head and looked for Sarke. But the tall black figure had moved several lengths ahead of him and was beating his horse cruelly while he screamed for the Children to exterminate the mutants forever.

David wanted to shut his eyes. He knew he was watching the end of the village and the death of the people he had grown to love.

Suddenly, in the path of Sarke, stood Willod. In his arms he held the sacred writings of Jahben. He stood straight and stared calmly at the dreaded army bearing down on him.

The Children began to slow their horses. "Kill the mutants," shouted Sarke, his voice trembling with rage and fury. But the army would not go forward. They began to exchange glances of apprehension. Sarke,

Sarke the all-knowing, had repeatedly told them how the mutants feared them and ran from them like the stupid herd animals they raised.

Yet here was a mutant who faced his death, who faced Sarke without fear, without weapons, holding only an armful of rotting paper. The Children became confused, and their swords dangled uselessly at their sides.

"Do you know who I am?" asked Sarke of the mutant before him.

Willod returned his stare evenly. He spoke calmly and without fear. "I know that you are the Black Regent. That you and your army have come from the mountain to kill the Demosee. But even if you kill me, these writings, the sacred writings of Jahben, will live. And someday Dahben, son of Jahben, will come from the mountain and kill you in turn."

·*Twenty eight*·

"That time is now!" said David in an even voice.

Sarke gave an angry hiss and spun about, slashing at Willod. As the sword cut across the man's chest, he released the papers he was clutching. A gust of wind blew them into a pile of burning straw. "The sacred writings," gasped Willod. "The sacred writings." He began digging into the fire with his hands, trying to pull out the flaming papers.

"Impostor!" screamed Sarke. "I am the one. I am the Prince."

"I am David Bennet."

"The Prince," murmured some of the Children. "It is our Prince."

"I am the Prince," shouted Sarke. "The spirit entered me, and now I and only I rule forever and ever. Kill him! I order you to kill him!"

But the Children did not obey. They looked fearfully at Sarke, but seemed unable to move.

"Very well," said Sarke, staring straight at David. In his voice there was the challenge of a death fight. David nodded, and both men dismounted.

The two approached one another and gave the formal combat bow before stepping back. "I could have easily killed you before," said Sarke. "If *she* hadn't distracted me."

"And I will kill you now, Sarke. You do not belong in this new world, and I will not let you infect it with your lies and your hate."

The fighting began. It was fierce and cruel and bloody. The Children and the Demosee stood waiting. The only sounds were the striking of sword against sword, and the occasional jingle of harness as horses stamped impatiently in the background.

As the fight continued, David found himself remembering the huge white combat room and Sarke's
laughter as he stumbled in exhaustion. Sarke was not
laughing now, but David's limbs were aching with
fatigue and already his sword arm throbbed painfully
as he parried the heavy strokes of the older man. Before he had fought in the white combat room with
Irene watching and fearing. Here there was only the
cold frozen ground of the reed swamp, the smell of
burning straw, and a ring of people, half of them mutants of the Time-After world and half of them beautiful but empty reminders of the Time-Before.

As David began to tire out, he realized that Sarke
probably would kill him. The man was stronger and
more experienced. Also, his strength and hatred had
grown with time, not lessened. Sarke's blade caught
his arm. There was the quiet snick of cloth and skin
tearing, and then the blood began its dark stain.

David felt no fear, only a sense of relief. It would
be over soon. Irene was lost forever. The Children
would exterminate the village. There was nothing left.
He had failed in everything. He saw the lights of his
house flicker in welcome, and the tree in his yard in
the full bloom of spring. When he stepped to the
front door, it would swing open and his mother and
father would stand holding out their arms to him. The
nightmare of his imprisonment at the will of Lady
Anastasia was over. He did not belong in this world

any more than did Sarke. "I just want to go home," he whispered, and moved his sword arm aside to leave his chest uncovered.

"So be it," snarled Sarke triumphantly.

The Demosee began to stir. "Dahben, Dahben, Dahben," they chanted in unison.

The Children began their own cry. "David, lead us. David, lead us."

Sarke whipped back his sword for the final killing thrust. For David the moment seemed to take centuries. He saw Sarke clearly. He saw the glint of light on steel. He heard the chanting of the Demosee and the Children. He saw himself climbing the stairs of his own house in the Time-Before. He saw the outstretched hands of his parents. He felt their love. There was a sound of wind at his back. In the wind came the faint chanting—"Dahben. David. Dahben. David. Dahben. David."

It was like a force pulling him back. The yard and the house and the tree dissolved into the smell and grayness of the reed swamps. As his father's image faded, David heard his voice. "No, my son, you must choose to live. Otherwise they will all die in darkness."

Jack Bennet's face dissolved. David felt a wave of disappointment and loss. Sarke stood over him. The bright sword of the Regent was thrusting down toward him with lightning speed. The man had thrown back his head and was laughing wildly in anticipation of the kill. He was no longer even looking at David. He was lost in his own madness.

In that split second of weakness, David flung himself toward Sarke, and before the man could step back or parry, he plunged his own sword straight into the Black Regent's chest. The laughter stopped, and a look of surprise passed over the man's face. He crumpled down, and his sword fell from his hand. As he lay on the ground, his eyes stared at the sky. His breaths were long and rasping.

The dark red blotch on his chest spread quickly. David knelt beside the dying man. "Irene," gasped Sarke. "She is mine." His words became faint. "I have loved her for . . . hundreds of years." Then his lips were still.

Willod looked at him from where the papers lay smoldering. "The sacred writings of Jahben," he said in an agonized voice. Only the leader could touch them.

"Are only words on paper," said David gently. He took one of the remaining scraps of document and held it up to the light. It was written in a familiar scrawl, but only a fraction remained legible.

. . . so much death and sickness here, and will be for years and generations to come. Will we ever right the wrong that we committed when we put our precious government, our free will into the hands of computers? At least the Guardians have destroyed themselves in their final fury. And my son, what advice can I give to you, if ever you wake from your unnatural imprisonment? How can I smooth the way for you? *[Here, a burn mark cut across the document.]*. . . . spent the last few moments of my time in the outside world trying to reach you. But I had to help the people, the people who stayed or were left behind. It's up to you to continue what I started. Help them to use their free will wisely, and to believe in that which lies beyond computers and machines. Do not sow the seeds for a second destruction. *[Another burn mark.]*. . . .in spite of logic and what the Guardians would have us think, my love for you will reach across the years, and even when you too are dead, my love for you and your dear mother will live on.

Here the paper became torn and illegible. David felt the tears streaming down his face. He turned away and looked over the frozen wasteland. "My father," he whispered.

He folded the fragment of burned paper and carefully put it in the folds of his tunic, close to his chest.

"Dahben," murmured Willod in an awed voice. He sank to his knees.

"No," said David with a gentle smile. "My father would not want that. Yes, I am the one you call Dahben. I am also the one they call the Sleeping Prince.

But I am neither. I am David Bennet, son of Jack
Bennet."

"Have you come to rule us with your wisdom?"
asked Willod humbly.

"No."

The crowd, both Children and villagers, gave a low
moan of disappointment.

"The way of the Demosee," David smiled as he
realized what the original word was, "is a good beginning. It is what my father would have wanted," he
added when he saw the confusion on their faces.

"So speaks Dahben, son of Jahben," intoned Willod solemnly.

The paralysis affecting both the villagers and the
Children was gradually dissolving. The Children had
moved into their own group, some staring at the dead
figure of Sarke in dull amazement. The villagers' anger was returning, and there was the sound of spears
being sharpened, and knives pulled from belts.

"No," said David sternly. "The true way of the
Demosee is a way of peace for all people."

"You killed Sarke," one of the Children said slowly.
"How will we know what are dreams and what are
not, without him?"

David glanced thoughtfully at them and then at
Willod. "Care for them," he said quietly. "As if they
were truly children. They have a sickness of the mind.
Sarke has controlled them for many years. But they

are not evil. And they will heal in time and become
part of the Demosee. The time of killing is over!"
He mounted his horse and gathered the reins.

"You are leaving us?" asked Willod.

David nodded. "For a while. I want to be alone."
He rode his horse slowly away, feeling the stares of
the Children and the Demosee at his back.

·*Twenty nine*·

David let the horse choose her own path, and she
wandered slowly back to the castle she knew. But the
castle was empty now. Even the slaves seemed to
have crept away.

He walked through deserted corridors, through areas
of the castle used by the Children, and through whole
sections that had crumbled into decay, where pillars
lay broken and covered in ancient dust. Sarke was
dead, Irene had proved empty, just a mouthpiece for
Mommy, incapable of change or learning. His anger
was replaced with loss. He would in time return to
the village. But for now, a feeling of despair had settled over him. He heard nothing but his own footsteps and the hollow sound of his own breath.

At last he found himself on the high monkswalk at

the top of the castle, where he had first met Triad, where Willard had followed him to escape, and from where he and Irene had fled on that last day. The arches of the walk had crumbled, and the surrounding wall was nothing but rubble. Suddenly he stared in surprise. He was not alone.

A figure was kneeling on the cold ground. Her white gown rippled in the wind. She had gathered a handful of dust in one hand, and was watching the grains dance on the breeze.

"Irene?"

She looked up. "David!" she said, smiling cautiously.

"Where's Mommy?" he asked coldly.

"She's dead."

David took a deep breath. "What are you going to do now?"

Irene stood up quickly. Her eyes were clear and her hair flowed in golden waves. She spoke urgently. "I saved the secrets. I know I hurt you and I'm sorry. But I could not let them be destroyed or lost forever. I risked everything for them, David, even you. And that was the hardest of all." The wind blew her hair back, and it glinted in the sun. As her cape moved, David could see about her neck many curious garlands with carved metal cases between the jewels and twisted gold wires. She broke off a tiny case and handed it to him. "Be very careful. These are the most precious things in the world," she cautioned.

He snapped the seal, there was a hiss of escaping air, and several small brown seeds fell into his hand.

"My secrets," Irene said, and smiled softly.

"Seeds?" he asked, uncomprehending, and then finally he understood. A feeling of gladness and awe swept over him.

"Yes," she answered in a low voice. "I had a garden once with many flowers and fruit trees." Hesitantly, David moved closer to Irene until their fingers touched and slowly became intertwined.

Hand in hand, they stared over the desolate reed swamps, each remembering what had been before.

Pueri omnia vicent

· *Deborah Moulton* ·

began her storytelling career answering the demands of her children for stories "from her imagination." Her first book, *The First Battle of Morn*, was a gripping fantasy set on a far-off world. Now she is back to Earth for *Children of Time*, a chilling, suspenseful tale of the future.

Ms. Moulton lives in Oyster Bay, New York, with her husband and two children.